THE FILE ON COLONEL MORAN:
SHERLOCK HOLMES
TAKES A HAND

An exciting trio of tales following the escapades of Colonel Sebastian Moran, 'one of the best shots in the world' and the 'second most dangerous man in London', according to Sherlock Holmes. Find out how Moran achieves his position at the right hand of Professor Moriarty in *The Hurlstone Selection*; shares lodgings with Holmes, Watson, and Mrs Hudson in *The Man with the Square-Toed Boots*; and turns his skills to art theft in *The Disappearance of Lord Lexingham*.

VERNON MEALOR

THE FILE ON COLONEL MORAN: SHERLOCK HOLMES TAKES A HAND

Complete and Unabridged

LINFORD
Leicester

First published in Great Britain

First Linford Edition
published 2014

A catalogue record for this book is available
from the British Library.

ISBN 978–1–4448–1870–3

Published by
F. A. Thorpe (Publishing)
Anstey, Leicestershire

Set by Words & Graphics Ltd.
Anstey, Leicestershire
Printed and bound in Great Britain by
T. J. International Ltd., Padstow, Cornwall

This book is printed on acid-free paper

*To my wife Kathleen and
our
daughter Helen.*

Introduction

Moran, Sebastian, Colonel. Unemployed. Formerly 1st Bangalore Pioneers. Born London, 1840. Son of Sir Augustus Moran, C. B., once British Minister to Persia. Educated Eton and Oxford. Served in Jowaki Campaign, Afghan Campaign, Charasiab (despatches), Sherpur, and Cabul. Author of Heavy Game of the Western Himalayas (1881); Three Months in the Jungle (1884). *Address: Conduit Street. Clubs: The Anglo-Indian, the Tankerville, the Bagatelle Card Club.*

'The Adventure of the Empty House',
Arthur Conan Doyle, 1902

★   ★   ★

University research can be dull and plodding at the best of times, so when a project comes along that intrigues and stimulates, it has to be welcomed with open arms. That's what I felt when it was suggested

1

that the life of Colonel Sebastian Moran could make a fascinating study. I was already familiar with the basic facts about the man and had often wondered what could have motivated someone of his unique abilities to take on the role of deputy to such a criminal mind as Professor Moriarty. Now I had an opportunity to delve deeply into the colonel's true character and I took advantage of it right away. I learned that 'the second most dangerous man in London' was in fact interviewed by a reporter named Mark Jordan while awaiting his trial for the murder of the Honourable Ronald Adair. Moran's tales of his life with Moriarty document a series of adventures which parallel those of Sherlock Holmes and Dr Watson, and it is my pleasure to reproduce them as they first appeared in *The Daily News* in the spring of 1894. My only concern is that the planned weekly series is incomplete, from which I deduce that the colonel either escaped or was released from prison.

Vernon Mealor
Southend-on-Sea, June 2010

The Hurlstone Selection

The autumnal sunshine filtered gently through the top pane of the only window in Colonel Moran's living room at 221C Baker Street. This limited illumination was the one disadvantage of his basement apartment, as the low brick wall outside blocked any view through the lower pane, giving him an oblique view of the day-to-day activities in the street above. His vision of life on Baker Street, therefore, was limited to boots and shoes, horses' hooves and carriage wheels.

No matter, Moran was happy with his choice. It was quite centrally located and he was able to go as he pleased with no fear of interference from prying eyes. Mrs Hudson, his landlady, kept very much to herself and his independence was complete. Moriarty, too, had been comparatively quiet over the past month or so, since the little affair at Groverston Hall in July. He had, it is true, held one or two meetings to discuss strategy for his projects for the 1881 season starting in January, but nothing major was being planned for the last few months of the current year.

Moran spent a lot of time at his desk by the window, attempting to convert Moriarty's rather abstract schemes into the practical realities required for successful operations. Moriarty was putting much more responsibility on his shoulders now, gaining confidence in him, as he got to know him better. There was still much to learn of the devious operations of his world-wide criminal network, however, and Moran was well aware of the vital necessity of absorbing a great deal in a very short time, if he were to achieve his ambition to play a leading role in the organization.

The Hudson River Tunnel project in New York had been occupying his mind for some time. He had reached the stage of finalizing some key elements in the plan and was ready to write them down in presentable form for Moriarty's consideration. With this in mind he went over and sat down at his desk after lunch. He had just taken up his pen to begin the task, when his thoughts were suddenly interrupted by the clatter of wheels close by. A dark shadow fell across his page and a heavy object thudded down against his window pane.

Startled, he leapt to his feet, and looked over at the window. A pair of sightless eyes met his horrified gaze. The motionless body of a man lay stretched right across the window, completely blocking out the light. The neighing of horses and the sharp crack of a whip startled Moran into action.

It took him a few seconds to fling open his living room door, race up the stairs leading to the front door and rush out into the street, but, by the time he reached the window, the body had completely disappeared. Moran spun round, ran quickly into the middle of the street, and looked up and down. There was nothing to be seen in either direction. Only the rustling of the leaves along the pavements disturbed the eerie silence.

Moran stood stock-still. The speed with which the man had disappeared was impossible to believe, and yet there was the empty paved area in front of the window to prove it. Slowly he walked up to the window and bent down to examine the ground where the man had been lying. Nothing. It was just as though there had never been a body there at all.

Moran stood up, tugging hard at his moustache in frustration. He simply couldn't believe the evidence of his own eyes. With a deep sigh, he took another look around and then, realizing there was nothing more he could do, turned to go back indoors. As he did so, he suddenly caught sight of a small brown object, partly concealed under the railings along the wall. He leaned forward and picked it up. It was a leather purse and could have fallen out of the man's pocket as he fell to the ground. If so, it might contain a vital clue to the man's identity.

Slipping the purse into his pocket, Moran hurried back inside. He locked the door, went over to the table, and shook out the contents of the purse. There wasn't much in it — just a few coins, a key and an odd-looking medallion. He picked it up and scrutinized it carefully. It was intricately engraved with a series of small intersecting circles on a plain blue background. He took it over to the lamp to inspect it more closely. The regular pattern of the circles suggested it was more than just a decoration. It could be part of a heraldic design, although Moran's limited knowledge of English heraldry allowed him to progress no further with that line of reasoning. He was intrigued, to say the least, and determined to pursue the matter more fully the next day.

* * *

That night Moran's sleep was disturbed by recurring images of the strange incident of the previous evening and he woke up early, eager to try to find out just what lay behind it all. The medallion would indeed seem to be a good starting point and so, after a hasty breakfast, he walked round the corner to see if the reference section of the library could throw any light on the matter. On the way he passed the familiar one-legged news-paper vendor at his regular stand on the corner of the street and the headline on one of the billboards caught his eye: *Another Banker Vanishes*. Intrigued, he bought a copy of the *Star* and stopped to read the front page.

The story was sensational. Five leading London bankers had already disappeared during the past week shortly after leaving their homes and a sixth had not been seen since the previous evening. No trace of any of the missing men had been found. The police suspected kidnapping, but no ransom demands had been received, which suggested something much more serious. The disappearances were also being linked to a spate of bank robberies at various locations throughout the county.

How odd. He couldn't help feeling that this had all the hallmarks of the work of a highly organized gang and yet he knew of none operating. He prided himself on his knowledge of the movements of the criminal fraternity at any given time in London and he was disturbed by this development. A little investigation of his own was called for, he felt. If successful, it could only enhance his reputation in Moriarty's eyes, for he knew Moriarty could never countenance the existence of a rival organization on what he considered to be his territory.

He crossed the road, hailed a passing cab and was on the point of getting in when he remembered why he had come out and hesitated. 'First things first,' he muttered to himself. 'The gang can wait a while. They'll be deeply engrossed in their current venture for some time yet. I've a clue to follow, while it's hot.' He waved the cabbie on and continued to the library.

He spent some time poring over the bulky tomes on English heraldic coats of arms. Most were alphabetically arranged and two hours passed by before he had even approached the halfway stage. No success so far. It was beginning to appear a thankless task when he turned to the letter 'H' and came across a similar pattern of rings in the coat of arms of the Hurlstone family. The intricate pattern of the circles was undoubtedly similar, although the background was of a much more vivid hue than on the medallion. Still, that was something to work on perhaps and he quickly turned up the address of the Hurlstone family in another thick volume. Reference was made to a village in West Sussex with that name and Hurlstone Manor appeared to be the address of the local squire, Sir Reginald Musgrave.

He sat back in his chair and pulled at his moustache. West Sussex was a long way off and this could be a very wild goose chase. Nevertheless, this was the only clue he had and he just had to find out why someone would dump a body at his window. The thrill of the chase stirred once again in his veins, and the old *shikari* bared his teeth at the prospect.

A brief study of a Bradshaw on a nearby table produced details of a fast train to Hurlstone later that afternoon. That would give him adequate time to tidy up his notes on the Hudson River Tunnel project before leaving for the station. He pushed aside the pile of books he had accumulated, left the library, and headed back to his apartment, satisfied with the results of his research.

It had started to rain heavily while he was in the library. He had to pick his way gingerly through the puddles that had lodged in the cracks in the paving stones. The street was deserted now. Even the newspaper vendor had given up trying to sell his wares and gone off to find a dry spot to shelter in. There was a large area of thick mud near where he had been standing and Moran had to step round it carefully.

He couldn't help noticing that someone had been making patterns in the mud. Probably some children delighting in the opportunity the mud provided of playing a game in the street, he thought. Something about the drawings made him look more closely at them, however. The patterns were quite clearly arranged in blocks of interlinking circles, remarkably like the ones he had just been looking at in the library. He stopped for a moment, studying them in detail. Finally he shook his head. Pure coincidence. It couldn't be anything else. A children's game, without doubt.

Nevertheless, as he walked on, he couldn't help pondering over what was a remarkable coincidence. A vague feeling of unease came over him. He soon arrived back home and went up to the front door to put his key in the lock. Out of the corner of his eye, he suddenly became aware of an object leaning against his window. He went over to see what it was. It turned out to be a rather unusually shaped stick, round and thick, with a bowl-shaped attachment at one end. In fact, it looked very like the stump of a wooden leg, socket and all. He took hold of it to examine it more closely and, as he did so, a piece of paper it had been holding in place against the window fluttered to the floor.

It was folded into four. He opened it up and was amazed to find the words 'KEEP AWAY FROM HURLSTONE' written in large, bold, black letters. Who could possibly know what his intentions were? He had only learnt of the existence of the place a short while ago. The situation was growing more mysterious and intriguing every minute. It now seemed that the circles in the mud were not a coincidence after all. They were a message intended for him alone — but what was it? And what about the wooden leg? The reference was obviously to the newspaper vendor, but why? Pulling at his moustache in bewilderment, he tucked the stump under his arm and went into the apartment.

He placed the stump across one of the chairs, went over to the table and looked down at his papers. There was no way he could settle down to work on the Hudson River Tunnel project after all that had happened this afternoon; his mind was in a complete turmoil. Of one thing, however, he was completely certain. The warning he had received only served to fire up his hunting instincts. A challenge had been laid down and he could hardly wait to take it up. The arrival of his cab to take him to the station couldn't come quickly enough for him.

★ ★ ★

The journey to Hurlstone took longer than he had anticipated and darkness was already beginning to fall when he emerged from the little village station. A porter informed him that the manor house was a short walk through pleasant country lanes, so he set off briskly, glad of the exercise after a tedious train journey.

The narrow, winding lanes took him past cultivated fields of wheat and barley and the colourful hedgerows on either side gave off a variety of scents from the profusion of wild flowers. The buzzing of insects and the cries of birds heading for their nests filled the air. An agreeable background indeed, but, after half an hour's strenuous walking, the lanes seemed interminable. The manor house was further from the station than he had been given to believe. He had hoped to arrive before it dark, but it looked as if that wouldn't be possible. He wanted to find a spot to rest his weary legs, and spotted a grassy knoll just ahead to his right. He moved over and sat down heavily, stretching out his legs.

The moon had risen and everything

around him had taken on a different hue under its faint light. The sounds were different too. The familiar ones had ceased, but, through the silence of the night, a new one began to be heard: the steady clump of rhythmic digging, slow and regular, as if spades were cutting into soil. Moran looked to see where it might be coming from. Round the next bend, just beyond where he was sitting, a church steeple loomed up against the moonlight and it was from that direction that the sounds were most audible.

Moran stood up again, walked down the lane very quietly, and turned around the bend. He could see the church much more clearly now and beyond it the bulky outline of a large building, which he took to be Hurlstone Manor. The sound of digging was louder from here and he estimated that it was coming from close by the church. He drew nearer and looked over the hedge.

A strange sight met his eyes. Silhouetted against an irregular line of gravestones, several men were absorbed in digging around one of the graves that had sunk into the

15

ground from neglect. Pools of bright light from dark lanterns illuminated the area, revealing the piles of earth the men had dug up so far. A pile of large sacks lay to one side of the grave and, every now and then, one of the men would bend down, work something loose from deep below and put it in a sack.

The men seemed to know exactly what they were looking for as they dug deep into the earth. Some items were rejected and thrown to one side; others were wiped down carefully and placed in a special container. Bits of timber that must have come from a coffin were lifted up and placed to one side.

Moran was under no illusions about what he was witnessing. These were grave-robbers at work, plying their disgusting trade at dead of night. No doubt they would sell the most highly regarded of their findings to medical schools in the London area and be paid handsomely for their efforts. Repugnant as he found the work they were engaged in, there was no way Moran could try to stop it. The men looked a pretty rough bunch and would have had no trouble overpowering him, strong and fit though he was.

There was nothing for it but to leave them to their revolting task, so he turned and tiptoed away from the hedge. As he did so, he suddenly heard the sound of running footsteps approaching from the lane. He pressed himself as close to the hedge as possible and saw a young girl in obvious distress race past him, carrying a bag in her hand. She disappeared round the next bend as fast as she had come, her footsteps echoing.

So surprised was Moran that he failed to notice a shadow coming up rapidly from behind. A slight noise made him turn, but it was too late. Something heavy crashed down on his head and he fell to the ground. He heard the sound of whistles and feet pounding past before he lost consciousness.

★ ★ ★

When Moran finally opened his eyes, he felt completely disoriented. His head throbbed violently, as he struggled to

17

make out where he was. Indoors, of that he was certain, but where and how he had got there remained a complete mystery. He glanced around him. The bare walls suggested a cell of some kind and the steel door with its tiny shuttered window reinforced this idea. He was sitting on a kind of hard mattress in one corner and he slowly got up to stretch his legs. At that moment the sound of a key being turned in the lock brought him up short. The heavy door swung open and a constable walked in.

'Inspector Lestrade wants a word,' he said. 'Follow me.'

Moran shrugged his shoulders, went out of the cell, and followed the constable down a poorly lit corridor to a door at the end. A familiar voice called 'enter' in response to the constable's knock.

Lestrade was leafing through a thick wad of documents, as the constable ushered Moran into the room. 'Sit down,' he muttered without looking up, indicating a chair in front of his desk with a flick of his hand.

Moran glared at him, tugged at his

moustache, and sat down in the chair. He remembered his last meeting with Sergeant Lestrade — as he was then — at Groverston Hall and didn't relish another. Still, he would at least find out why he was being held in police custody. He waited in silence.

After a few moments Lestrade looked up from his papers and grinned. 'Well, you've done it this time, there's no mistake.'

Moran's bushy eyebrows shot up in amazement. You don't say,' he sneered, pushing his chair back a fraction and waiting for clarification.

'To be frank,' went on Lestrade, 'I hadn't thought of you as capable of this. Kidnapping, yes. You are, in my view, a prime suspect in the latest spate of kidnappings, but grave-robbing just didn't seem to be in your line.'

Moran sat bolt upright. 'What's that?' he gripped the arms of his chair until his knuckles turned white. 'Don't you go around thinking that promotion gives you the right to hurl wild accusations at innocent members of the public.'

'Wild accusations are they?' Lestrade bent down, picked up a large brown paper packet that was lying at his feet and threw it casually at Moran. 'You recognize that, I imagine.'

Moran caught it and looked down at it in surprise. 'No. I've never seen it before.'

'Open it,' said Lestrade, leaning forward to watch Moran closely as he opened the packet. There was no mistaking the look of absolute revulsion on Moran's face, when he saw what was inside. He threw the packet onto the floor.

'You had that with you when we found you in the cemetery,' went on Lestrade.

'If so, one of the grave-robbers must have put it there.' Moran lost confidence as he began to realize the seriousness of his position.

'You were about to escape with your share of the spoils, more like,' Lestrade said curtly.

'Interrogate the others. You'll soon see that I'm not one of them. They don't even know me,' broke in Moran.

'What others?' Lestrade looked away in

disgust. 'You were the only one we caught.'

'I can't believe it. An entire gang right there and you couldn't catch a single one. That'll go down really well with your superiors.'

'You forget that we have you, and you are more value to us than a string of nonentities.'

Moran leaned back in his chair, stroking his moustache. He was beginning to regain his composure. 'You'll find me a very small fish indeed. You'd better throw me back, before I begin to embarrass you. I have nothing to do with that revolting trade and nothing you can say will change that.'

'There's the evidence,' replied Lestrade calmly, pointing to the packet. 'What do you expect me to believe? You've hardly an unblemished record, you know.'

'Nevertheless, it's going to be difficult to make it stick in court,' went on Moran confidently. He paused for a moment, thinking hard. 'And what about the girl?'

'What girl? My men didn't report any female involvement.'

Moran described what he'd seen before

he was knocked to the ground.

'That was probably one of the servants from the manor. Sir Reginald's been having some trouble with his domestics of late, I hear.'

'It looked more serious than that to me,' remarked Moran. 'There was a desperate look on her face that suggested more than a mere disagreement.'

'Well, that's a new element, to be sure. It's the gang that concerns me. They've been desecrating graves all over this area for the past month and we always seem to arrive too late.'

'I can't think why you are telling me all this,' broke in Moran. 'It can't possibly concern me.'

'Because you were obviously involved with them on their latest job. You'll have to produce evidence to the contrary if you want to avoid a court case.' Lestrade closed the folder on his desk and leaned back in his chair.

'How do you expect me to do that, if I'm stuck here in a cell?' replied Moran.

'That's not my problem.' Lestrade rose.

'As far as I'm concerned, you're the first member we've caught red-handed and, with the evidence in that packet, I'll have no difficulty securing a conviction in court.' He signalled to the constable standing outside the door. 'Take him back to his cell. We'll have him before the magistrate in the morning.'

'You're making a big mistake,' snarled Moran, struggling in the grip of the brawny policeman who had laid hands on him. 'I'm innocent.'

* * *

Lestrade watched Moran's removal and then turned back to his papers. He picked up a document and threw it aside in frustration. 'The last thing I need is this latest development,' he muttered. 'As if I haven't enough to do with kidnapped bankers and bank robberies. My resources are stretched to the limit as it is. Promotion certainly isn't all it's cracked up to be, that's for sure.' With a deep sigh he turned his attention to his paperwork again.

He wasn't allowed to concentrate on it for long.

A commotion broke out in the corridor outside his room. A blast on a whistle and the sound of running feet made him leap to his feet and open his door. The constable was lying flat on his back near the cell door, a whistle stuck in his mouth and his right hand signalling towards the outer door. Moran was gone.

'Get after him,' shouted Lestrade, raising the alarm. 'All available men get after him quick.' Doors burst open and a stream of policemen raced out of the station, pulling on their jackets and cramming their helmets onto their heads. They quickly spread out into the surrounding lanes in pursuit of the fugitive.

Moran had quite a considerable start on them, but his figure could be seen outlined against the dawn light, racing along the lane towards the church.

'Take the short cut to the estate, in case he tries to take shelter there,' yelled Lestrade, emerging from the station. Some of the constables shot off in that direction, while others continued through the lanes.

* * *

Moran was indeed heading for the grounds of Hurlstone manor, hoping to find refuge for a few hours in one of the outhouses that he knew were a feature of large estates. He stopped to catch his breath at a turning in the lane and took the opportunity to look back down the hill to see if he was being followed. Groups of policemen were clearly visible dotted about the countryside, all heading in his direction. There was little time to lose. Moran turned and realized that he was quite near the estate. The church and the cemetery, where he had been attacked earlier that night, were once again on his right and — as he ran past — he couldn't help looking over the familiar hedge.

To his surprise, he saw several men bending over the same open grave. He stopped and tip-toed closer. They must have doubled back and resumed their activities, no doubt feeling certain the police would not come back again to the same place that night. They were obviously about to complete their task, but Moran was in time to witness a remarkable incident.

Two of the men bent down and lifted up a man's body that had been lying on the ground nearby. As they carried it to the grave, Moran recognized the man's features. He had last seen them pressed to the window of his flat in Baker Street. They lowered the body into the grave, while the others shovelled in soil and then tidied up the surface, replacing plants and shrubs to conceal what lay beneath.

Moran was aghast.

The digging had a dual function, then. Human remains were taken, but were replaced by the bodies of murdered men, mutilated to order no doubt. The bodies were unlikely to be found once buried in existing graves and, without a body to identify, no crime could be proved to have been committed. This operation had been well thought out indeed. Lestrade had said that graves were being des-ecrated all over the county. This could be the solution to the disappearance of the bankers he had read about. No wonder there had been no ransom demands. The bank robberies had provided all the cash that was needed. After that the bankers had no further value and were disposed of.

Moran's ruminations were interrupted by the men's rapid departure. A plan was already hatching in his fertile brain. One that would lead to the arrest of the gang and clear his name at the same time.

Darting from hedge to hedge and using all available natural cover, Moran kept the men in view as they made their way into the grounds of the manor from deep in the estate. He made sure that his every move could be clearly seen by the irregular line of police closing up on him from the lanes below. By following him they would have the extra bonus of being able to round up the entire gang once he had discovered their meeting place.

Running into the grounds of the estate, the men headed for a dilapidated building that looked like an old barn. When the last man had gone in, Moran left his cover, gave a final glance behind him to see how far off the police were and ran round to the back of the barn. He found a small door leading to a long narrow wooden staircase, which he went up with those smooth cat-like movements so typical of him.

At the top the stairway opened out onto a wide balcony and Moran found himself looking down on the whole gang relaxing after their efforts. Bottles of beer and plates of food had been placed on long, wooden tables and the men were taking full advantage of them. Sir Reginald would be surprised to know what went on in this barn at night. Moran stroked his moustache. Two of the men were standing just below him, discussing the night's activities. Snatches of their conversation drifted up to him as he crouched, pressed against the edge of the balcony.

'If the other units have been as successful as ours, that should keep the police busy. The bank robberies have apparently gone well. The money will have been distributed, before the police realize what is happening . . . '

One of the men reached across the table for a bottle of wine and, his coat-sleeve rolled back to reveal a vivid red mark on his wrist: a triangle set inside a circle — the sign of the Scowrers, the feared American criminal organization. What were they doing so far from home? A rival gang operating in England wasn't something Moriarty would tolerate.

'I've got to let him know right away,' Moran whispered to himself.

He overheard another snatch of conversation. 'I need further instructions. Stay here with the rest of the boys, while I get to town to report to Number One.'

'Right, Hank, I'll take over. Get back as soon as you can, though.' Hank nodded, put down his glass and headed for the door.

Moran turned and raced down the stairs the way he had come. With any luck, Hank would lead him directly to the gang's headquarters, and then he would be in a position to provide Moriarty with a complete report. He ran out of the barn and was just in time to see Hank disappearing around the back of the manor house. Moran followed, stopping short when he heard the neighing of a horse and the rumble of wheels.

Hank was driving a dog-cart down the path towards the gates.

Moran's face fell. Without transport, he had no chance of catching him up. He raced round to the front of the manor house, but there was no dog-cart to be found. He saw all his hopes of clearing up the mystery vanishing in a second. He sat down on a bench under the enormous oak tree in front of the manor house, holding his head in his hands.

Suddenly Moran caught the sound of horses' hooves in the lane beyond the gates. He sprang to his feet and — to his delight — a four-wheeler turned into the drive and approached the manor house. He hid behind the trunk of the oak and waited. He couldn't believe his luck. He watched while a young man, attired in a grey travelling cloak and a cloth cap, stepped down, paid the cabbie and, strode up to the main entrance.

Moran came out from behind the tree and approached the driver. 'You passed a dog-cart on your way in. Follow it as fast as you can.' He leapt into the cab and was heading at full speed down the drive a moment later. As he passed through the gates, Moran looked back and gave a little smile of satisfaction at the sight of the police throwing a cordon around the barn. 'That's one unit disposed of anyway,' he muttered under his breath. The cab had left the drive, turned into the familiar lane and sped off in the direction the dog-cart had taken.

After a few minutes, Moran caught sight of the dog-cart in the distance and realized they were in danger of catching it up. He told the cabbie to slow down a little. 'It's vitally important that the man in the dog-cart doesn't realize he's being followed. Just keep him in view, but stay at a discreet distance.' The lanes were almost deserted at this early hour and Hank was certain to notice the hansom in the distance. He had no reason to think it was anything other than a routine fare, however, so Moran felt quietly confident that he would not suspect anything.

There was something hypnotic about the clip-clop of the hooves along the winding lanes. Moran found it difficult to keep awake, despite being aware of the importance of keeping alert while on his mission. He thought he could hear a different rhythm of hooves coming from behind. He turned to look back, but nothing was visible for miles, so he assumed he had imagined the sound. He shook his head vigorously and made a great effort to keep his eyes fixed on the road ahead.

He must have dozed off for a while because the next time he looked ahead there was no sign of the dog-cart. 'Driver, have we lost him?' The driver replied that the dog-cart must still be ahead as it hadn't left the road. Moran was furious with himself for falling asleep. Once again he had lost the chance to get to the bottom of the affair, this time through his own weakness of character. He looked around desperately. They were approaching a wayside inn and he told the driver to slow down to give him a good view of the carriages lined up outside. It was just possible that the dog-cart might be amongst them.

As luck would have it, Moran caught a glimpse of Hank coming out of the inn and heading for his cart.

Moran breathed a sigh of relief, his plans on track again.

He told the cabbie to drive slowly to allow the dog-cart to pass, which it did after about a hundred yards. The hunt was on again and this time Moran was determined that there would be no more mistakes. It took about two more hours of fast driving through the leafy lanes of Sussex and Surrey before they reached the streets of London and headed for the East End. A deserted warehouse turned out to be their destination. Moran had his cab wait some distance away, watching to see what Hank would do. He obviously knew his way about, as he went straight to a side door and vanished up a flight of stairs.

Moran paid the driver, leapt out of the cab, and raced around the building, looking for another entrance. He found a half-open door right round the back and went straight in. He found himself in a vast open space crammed with packing crates and a variety of other items ready for loading and — to judge by the labels

— shipping to all parts of the world. He tip-toed through the maze of wooden boxes and finally came to what appeared to be a large office area at the far end.

A lamp was burning in a window up on the top floor and he could see figures moving about silhouetted against the blind. He guessed that was where Hank had gone, so he crept up a nearby flight of stairs, until he came to a door with a lighted panel on top. He pushed it open gently and was mortified when the hinges creaked loudly. A tall figure of a man was standing with his back to him, as he stopped to take in the scene. Slowly the man turned to face Moran.

Moran made out a familiar face in the semi-gloom. 'Moriarty,' he gasped, stepping back into the doorway.

Moriarty smiled at him. 'Whom did you expect, old man? You should know by now that I'm always to be found at the centre of the web, spinning my plots like the industrious spider that I am.'

Moran was so taken aback that he could hardly stammer out a reply. 'But what about the Scowrers? I saw them at work with my own eyes.'

'I make use of anyone and anything to achieve my ends,' replied Moriarty, his head swaying gently. 'A disreputable mob like the Scowrers was essential if I was to succeed in filling our much depleted coffers.' He turned away and glanced to his right. 'Now the project has been completed, I can dispense with them, as Hank here has just realized. Their boss is already in jail, so his journey here was quite fruitless.'

Moran followed his glance and saw Hank standing with a revolver pointed at Moriarty.

'You talk too much,' growled Hank, gesturing to Moran to come forward into the light. 'You, get over there by the wall.'

Moriarty took advantage of this momentary distraction to step a little closer to a nearby table. He looked at Moran. 'You arrived just in time to witness the rapid departure of another member of the gang,' he hissed, pressing a concealed button set in the table-top.

A trapdoor dropped open under Hank's feet.

With a horrified cry, he vanished from our sight deep into the Thames.

Moran stood open-mouthed at the speed with which the tables had been turned.

'Good riddance,' snarled Moriarty, pressing the button again to close the trap door. He rubbed his hands together, walked over to a side-table, picked up a bottle of sherry and poured out two glasses.

Moran recovered his composure and sat down at the table. 'Now you've got some explaining to do. I get the point of all the murders, the secret burials and bank robberies, but what about the body thrown at my window and the business with wooden legs and mysterious circles? It got me involved, but how does it fit into the picture?'

Moriarty's mouth twisted into a grin. He held out a glass of sherry and said, 'Just a test. Part of my training programme for new recruits — and you are relatively new to my organization, are you not?' He sipped his drink, his head oscillating gently from side to side. 'I had to see how you would face up to a real challenge.'

Moran almost choked. 'Some training programme. I could have got myself killed.' He turned away in disgust.

'Ah, but you didn't and that was the whole point. In fact you came through it rather well, disposing of the Hurlstone unit quite neatly while my men were dealing with the rest of the gang.' A muffled noise from the corridor outside made Moriarty turn his head abruptly. 'You may even have done too well.' He stood up, pushing back his chair. 'I suspect Lestrade and his merry men have followed you here.'

Moran pulled himself to his feet with a great effort. He was beginning to tire of being pursued, and the strain showed on his face.

Moriarty roared with laughter and slapped him on the back. 'Quick, through this side-door and down the passage. It leads to the street.'

Moran paused, cast a bemused glance at Moriarty and followed him into the passage. He could hear footsteps in the corridor, and then a loud hammering on the door.

'There's a dog-cart waiting at the corner,' explained Moriarty, pushing open a gate at the end of the passage. 'Our escape has been carefully planned, as you see. After all, it would never do to have the two top men in my organisation in police custody, would it?'

Moran stopped for a moment, while the full significance of Moriarty's words sank in. Then he drew himself up to his full height, stroked his moustache in triumph, and followed Moriarty out to safety.

The Man With the Square-Toed Boots

Colonel Moran awoke with a start. All was silent in the room around him, but something unusual must have happened to disturb him. Not that he was a heavy sleeper. Too many nights exposed to the varied dangers of the African and Asian jungles had seen to that. He listened hard. There it was again. He could distinctly hear the pounding of feet coming from the staircase leading to the flat above. Then the banging of the front door, as someone left in a great hurry. Moran leapt out of bed, ran into the front room and up to the narrow window, which gave him a limited view of Baker Street. Nevertheless, he could make out small figures emerging from the house and disappearing up the street in the light of the dawn. The coarse jargon of street urchins was clearly audible for a few moments.

Moran turned from the window and sighed. This wasn't the first time he had been disturbed in the early hours of the morning by visitors to the flat above and it really was getting too much. He decided to speak to his landlady, Mrs Hudson, the next time he saw her. It wasn't like this when he had first come to live in 221C last year. The only other apartment in the building, 221B, was unoccupied. Moran could remember the exact date of the change: January 19th 1881 . . .

★   ★   ★

Moran was returning from a meeting with Moriarty when he saw trunks and bags carried through the front door, followed by a stockily-built man of about thirty, clinging to a leash on which a podgy bull-pup was straining. Moran waited on the other side of the street for a while before entering. The removal men were just taking the final items through the door of 221B when he went down the stairs to his basement apartment. He thought it would be pleasant to have a fellow lodger in the building, but he had more important things on his mind, a comparative analysis of the various projects Moriarty had brought up at their meeting.

The next morning a ring at the front-door bell had woken Moran early. The thud of more trunks being dragged over the threshold told him that another lodger had arrived. He couldn't resist having a quick look to see who his new neighbour was. He climbed from his bed, and opened his door a little. A tall young man with a cloth cap and a travelling cloak was ascending the stairs to 221B. It was only a fleeting glimpse, but Moran felt there was something familiar about him.

He closed the door and thought for a moment. Suddenly it came to him. It was the same person he had observed getting out of the cab at Hurlstone Manor a few months before. He shrugged his shoulders and stroked his moustache, surprised at the coincidence, and then put all thoughts of his new neighbour out of his mind.

Moran was fully occupied all day, drawing up detailed plans for the organisation's activities. By tea-time he had made such good progress that he felt he could legitimately take a break. He got up from the table, stretched his limbs, and went over to the window to see if the weather would permit a short stroll. The sun was shining and he was about to put on a lighter jacket when he became aware of someone strolling casually along the other side of the street.

Only the trouser legs and boots were visible, given the restricted view from the window, but that was enough to stimulate his curiosity. The well-worn, baggy trousers didn't match up with the pair of square-toed boots in the very latest fashion. Intrigued, Moran forgot all about his walk and kept his eyes on the view outside. The boots disappeared out of his line of vision, but then reappeared pointing in the opposite direction. A few moments later, they did the same thing again, retracing their steps.

The stranger was obviously either waiting for someone or watching the houses. It would do no harm to try to find out which, thought Moran. He left his room, raced up the stairs, opened the front-door, and went out into the street. He was puzzled to find it deserted. He walked a little way up towards the park and looked around carefully. There was no trace of the stranger.

Disappointed, Moran went back into the house. If the man had a reason for taking up a position in Baker Street, then he'd be back, and next time he wouldn't get away so easily. As he went down the stairs, he glanced up at his new neighbours' apartment. All was quiet behind the door. Moran thought how fortunate he was to have such considerate neighbours. He should have no trouble getting on with his work undisturbed, just as he had before they moved in.

All changed the following morning, however. Moran had just come in through the front door after an early morning stroll, when an excruciating screech rang out from the apartment above. It sounded like a bow violently clashing against the strings of a violin. It was augmented by

43

the howling of a dog and a frenzied scratching of claws on the side of a door. Suddenly the door was thrown open and a bull-pup hurtled down the stairs, yelping and barking with its tail firmly between its legs. Moran had to press himself close to the wall to avoid being knocked down by the maddened creature charging by.

Moran hadn't had time to close the front door and the dog raced straight out, barking and yelping as it disappeared down the street. The door to 221B slammed shut and peace reigned once more in the house. Moran leaned against the wall and wiped his brow with the white handkerchief he always kept in his sleeve. He tugged at his moustache, and closed the front door quietly. Mrs Hudson rushed in from the back of the house in great agitation. Moran assured her that everything was under control and there was no need to worry. Then he turned away, and went down the stairs to his own apartment . . .

From that moment on, things were never the same in the house. A steady stream of visitors to the apartment above came and went at all times of the day and night. Once he had got used to the new rhythm of life about him, Moran was, admittedly, intrigued to see the kind of people invited upstairs and he began to spend more time than he cared to remember at his window, deducing what he could from the steady stream of shapely ankles, hob-nailed boots, military uniforms, elegant shoes, and gaitered legs that flowed like a swirling tide before him.

What possible connection could there be between all those remarkably different types of humanity? And what kind of a man would be interested in meeting them? One of the residents in 221B must indeed be keen to encounter society in all its manifestations, but what on earth could be the purpose behind it? As Moran turned to his morning ablutions, he decided to find out for himself rather than complain to Mrs Hudson. The only problem was how to go about it.

★   ★   ★

The following morning provided a solution. Moran had decided on a frontal attack — marching up the stairs, rapping on the door, and introducing himself, but he didn't want to call on his neighbours if they were about to have guests. He went over to the window to see if anyone was approaching the house. At first it seemed there was no-one in sight, but then a familiar pair of square-toed boots came into view, moving slowly past on the other side of the street. As Moran watched, they reversed direction and went back, just as they had before.

So, the stranger had returned and taken up his position again. Moran stroked his moustache. Perhaps the new tenants had also become aware of the movements of the stranger in front of the house. That could be the reason for his unannounced visit. They might even be able to offer some kind of explanation to clear the whole thing up. Encouraged by this thought, he put on his jacket and went upstairs to 221B.

He knocked tentatively at the door and waited. Almost immediately the door opened, revealing a stockily-built man, whom Moran recognized as the first of the tenants to arrive.

'Ah. Good morning,' he said warmly, holding out his hand to Moran. 'My name's Watson, Dr Watson. We didn't expect you quite so soon, but do come in all the same.'

Moran opened his mouth to reply, but was ushered in before he had time to say a word.

A tall, thin man in his late twenties was standing in one corner of the room, bending over what looked like a motley collection of chemical apparatus on a large, cluttered table. He waved his hand without looking up.

'Take a seat. I'll be with you in a moment.'

'But I — ' began Moran.

'Shush, don't interrupt. Mr Holmes is engaged in a delicate chemical experiment. When I tell you that the life of a man may hang upon the result, you'll see how important it is. Here, sit down in the chair by the window while you are waiting.' Watson pulled an easy chair round to give Moran a good view through the bay window, and went over to a desk in the opposite corner of the room, where he began writing in a journal.

Moran sat in the chair as instructed. He gazed out of the window to while away the time. It provided a superb vista of the whole length of Baker Street, which was packed with pedestrians, carriages and cabs at this time of day. Moran's attention was soon drawn to the figure of a man pacing slowly up and down in front of the house. It was the first time he had been able to get a good look at the stranger and he leaned forward to observe him. The shabby trouser legs now so familiar to Moran were matched by an equally shabby brown coat and peaked cap. He was a thick-set, rather aggressive-looking individual, whose head twitched furtively as he continued his vigil. The fashionable, square-toed boots were still very much in evidence.

'Success!'

The exultant shout startled Moran from his reverie.

'Just the result I had hoped for.' The

tall man turned, a triumphant look on his face and a smoking test-tube clutched firmly in his hand. 'Ah.' He glanced over at Moran, as if suddenly aware of his presence in the room. 'Sorry about the delay. With you in a moment.' Holmes put the test-tube down carefully in a wooden rack on the table and went over to a nearby washstand, where he scrubbed his hands thoroughly in a bowl of hot water. He dried his hands with a towel, pulled up a chair directly opposite Moran, and looked closely at him, his keen eyes absorbing every detail.

Moran leaned back, puzzled.

'Let's see,' began Holmes. 'You've been in Africa, I perceive. Hmm. You saw service in the Army. A professional soldier. Rose to high rank, too. Then, back in civilian life, big-game hunting for pleasure. Some musical skills, though not practised of late.' His piercing eyes swept across Moran's astonished features. 'Over the past year somewhat troubled by attentions from the police.' Holmes' voice had dropped to a whisper now, as though he were talking to himself. 'Spent a little time in prison, but adjusting once more to life outside the bars. Still tempted by the attractions of, let us say, irregular activities, however. Not a conventional life, I venture to suggest, but one that craves excitement and adventure.' He sat back in his chair with a grunt of satisfaction.

Moran half rose, bristling with indignation as a deep flush spread over his cheeks. 'Really!' he gasped. 'What gives you, a perfect stranger, the right to — '

Watson rushed over and urged him to sit down, smiling at his confusion. 'Don't take offence, please. Mr Holmes' powers of observation are so finely developed that he takes every opportunity to practise them, completely forgetting the startling effect this can have on a stranger.'

'That's all very well,' spluttered Moran, 'but really, I came here on a purely charitable mission and I'm subjected to a gratuitous display of amateur character analysis. I think I've a right to object.'

Holmes looked up quickly. 'Charitable mission, did you say?'

'Well, perhaps a social visit is more

appropriate,' replied Moran. 'Your remarkable powers of observation let you down there, I'm afraid. I'm your neighbour from the apartment below and I called to introduce myself.'

Holmes looked nonplussed for a moment, then let out a great guffaw of laughter. 'It seems I definitely got beyond myself this time, Watson. I was expecting somebody else, sir. I do apologize most sincerely and I hope you will forgive my enthusiasm for the little tricks of my profession. My name is Holmes, Sherlock Holmes and you've already met my colleague, Dr John Watson.' He rose to shake Moran's hand.

'Moran, Colonel Sebastian Moran.' He took the outstretched hand.

'Have a glass of sherry with us,' urged Watson, going over to a side-table and pouring out three glasses. 'Let's start again on a more convivial basis.'

Moran gave a smile, smoothed his moustache and, went over to take a glass.

They drank each other's health warmly.

Moran said he would have to leave in a few moments, as he had a business appointment later that morning, but, drew Holmes' attention to the stranger outside the building, wondering if he knew anything about him.

Holmes looked at him with interest. 'A stranger, you say. No, I've been so absorbed in my experiments that I can't remember when I last looked out of the window.' With that, he strolled over.

Moran and Watson joined him.

The stranger was still there, walking up and down as before.

'Ah,' mused Holmes, staring at him. 'Do you mean that ex-middle-weight boxer over there? Hmm, that was just a hobby, I perceive.' Holmes' voice dropped to a whisper again. 'Bank clerk by profession, well thought of by his colleagues, promoted to a high position, but then . . . ah. The frailty of the human condition. He succumbed to temptation and a criminal record ensued. He has known bad times, but is currently enjoying prosperity again, though making every attempt to conceal it.' With a yawn, Holmes turned away. 'Apart from those trifles, I can deduce nothing about the man, I'm afraid. If he continues to loiter, however, I can procure swift action from the police.'

'Remarkable, Holmes,' exclaimed Watson. 'Quite remarkable.'

Holmes opened his mouth to comment.

'Don't say it,' implored Watson vehemently.

Holmes glanced at him. 'Perhaps you're right.' He nodded. 'Yes, perhaps you're right.'

Stunned by this further display, Moran shook his head and made his way to the door. He turned as a thought struck him. He looked over at Holmes, who had resumed his place at the chemical table. 'You mentioned a profession a little while ago, Mr Holmes. I would be very interested to hear what it is.'

Holmes paused for a moment, peering closely at a test-tube in his hand. 'Let's say I try to help people who come to see me with their little problems.' He put down the tube and leaned over the table towards some boxes of chemicals in preparation for his next experiment.

Realizing he would get no more information from Holmes, Moran said goodbye, and made his way down the stairs to his own apartment, reflecting on the curious behaviour he had witnessed that morning. Holmes certainly possessed the most sensitive and acute powers of observation, but Moran failed to see how this faculty could be developed into a full-time profession. He had little time to ponder more deeply on the problem, however, as he had to prepare for an important meeting with Moriarty. The new project they were to finalize at the meeting could well take him abroad and he had a selection of maps of Europe to take with him.

When everything was ready, Moran gathered all the relevant documents from the table, placed them in a valise together with the maps, put on his overcoat, and left the apartment. He must have been unusually quiet going up the stairs and opening the front door, because right opposite him on the other side of the street stood the solitary figure of the stranger who had been pacing up and down earlier that morning.

At the unexpected sight of Moran, he turned on his heels and ran up the street as fast as he could go. Sensing an opportunity to find out who he was and what his motives were, Moran put down his valise in the hallway and raced after him. It didn't turn out as easily as he had expected. The stranger obviously knew his way about that part of London, darting up narrow alleyways and leaping over adjoining walls. Fit though he was, Moran just couldn't match his speed and fell further and further behind. Finally he gave up the chase and returned to the house.

As he approached, Moran was surprised to see Sherlock Holmes standing outside the front door.

'I was just coming downstairs, when I saw you run off after that fellow, so I've been standing guard over your valise,' explained Holmes. 'You never know who might come by.'

'That was very thoughtful of you,' replied Moran. 'Thank you very much. I'm afraid I forgot everything in the heat of the chase. He got away, though.'

'Ah,' murmured Holmes, waving his hand in farewell, as he turned to walk down the street.

Moran hailed a passing cab to take him to Moriarty's. The short journey gave him the chance to catch his breath and compose himself for the meeting. This was to be a crucial one for him, because it would be his first project since his promotion to chief of staff of the organisation, and he wanted to make an especially good impression. On arrival he was shown straight into Moriarty's lounge, where there were five men busy at work on documents that Moriarty had distributed. Moran knew them all by sight and greeted them.

He realized they had been hand-picked for the job being planned. Ben and Joe were very similar in build, small, wiry, and agile. Albert and Sam were of a different calibre: tall, strong, heavily-built with rather dull, coarse features. Fred, on the other hand, was a suave individual with hair carefully brushed back and a neat, black moustache. Despite their physical differences, they were all alike in one respect: they were all experts in their chosen fields.

Moran took a seat at the table and

waited for Moriarty to come in. Almost immediately a door at the end of the room opened and Moriarty appeared, accompanied by a rather shabby, portly individual with thinning grey hair and a grizzled moustache.

'Ah, good to see you again, Moran,' he said, his head oscillating from side to side. 'You haven't met Slim yet, have you?' He beckoned to his companion to come forward and put his hand on his shoulder. 'I've brought Slim over from his base in Zurich, because of his inside knowledge of the Swiss banking system. You'll be working closely with him on our latest project.' He turned to look at Slim. 'This is Colonel Moran, my chief of staff.'

Slim came up and shook hands with Moran. 'Very pleased indeed to make your acquaintance.' His voice was deep and rasping, and his podgy cheeks quivered as he pumped Moran's hand.

'Welcome to London,' said Moran. 'I look forward to working with you.' Even as he uttered these words a vague feeling of unease came over him. Slim went across to take a seat at the table. Moran watched him go and the feeling of unease grew stronger. They had met before, he was sure of that, but where? He stared hard at the shabby coat and baggy trousers and a thought suddenly struck him. He shook his head and grinned. It was too outrageous for words, so he dismissed it from his mind.

Moriarty called the meeting to order and Moran sat down and put his papers in front of him ready for the discussion to begin. Moriarty presented the plan clearly and thoroughly and then each man made his contribution, asking for various clarifications of the details. Unusually, Moran found his concentration beginning to waver, his thoughts wandering to Slim's strangely familiar appearance. Then an idea came to him, which might clear the whole thing up. He dropped one of his papers on the floor, bent down to pick it up and caught a glimpse of Slim's boots. Any lingering doubts he might have had about Slim's identity were dispelled at what he saw.

A pair of fashionable square-toed boots were protruding from the baggy trouser legs. Slim and the stranger outside the house in Baker Street were one and the same man. Moran sat upright in his chair and glanced at Slim, but no sign of recognition disturbed his impassive features. From then on the discussion proceeded for Moran as if it were a distant murmur. His concentration was constantly interrupted by flashes of those square-toed boots and baggy trousers outside the house.

The more he thought of it, however, the more his doubts began to surface. Could he have been mistaken? After all, there must be many men going about with fashionable, square-toed boots . . . but wouldn't they wear stylish clothing to match? If it were Slim, then it must presumably be on Moriarty's instructions, which raised the question of why Moriarty would want to spy on a faithful lieutenant like himself? He couldn't wait for the meeting to end, so he could bring the matter up with Moriarty.

'So, we are agreed,' Moriarty disturbed his reverie, 'Target: the *Loewen und Daumen* Private Bank. Address: *Maehnestrasse*, Zurich, Switzerland. Date:

Saturday February 26th 1881. Are there any final questions?' Moriarty looked hard at each face in turn. 'Right. Meeting concluded. You all know your duties. Carry them out well and we'll pull off the robbery of the year. The very best of luck to you.'

The five men got up from the table and went to Moriarty one by one to thank him for all he had done and to say farewell. Slim shook his hand silently, smiled, and followed the men out of the room. Moran waited until the door had closed and then he turned to Moriarty, who was tidying up his papers on the table.

Moriarty looked up. 'Excellent meeting, eh?'

Moran agreed. 'With such precise planning, this operation should run very smoothly indeed. I'll leave for Zurich at the beginning of next week to liaise with our Swiss colleagues. You can rely on me, you know that.'

Moriarty slapped him on the shoulder amiably. 'You don't need to tell me that.'

Moran glared at him. 'Then why, may I ask, are you having me watched?'

'Watched? What on earth are you talking about? I'm not interested in your movements.' Moriarty seemed genuinely surprised.

'I've spotted someone looking very much like Slim outside my apartment in Baker Street several times lately. Don't tell me he was there just for the benefit of his health.' Moran pulled at his moustache angrily.

'So that's it.' Moriarty's brow cleared. 'I'd completely forgotten you now live in Baker Street. It was Slim you saw, all right, but his assignment wasn't what you thought. Come over by the fire, sit in one of the chairs, and I'll tell you all about it.' He took a seat.

Relieved at this comment, Moran sat down opposite Moriarty.

The professor remained silent for a while, staring at the blazing coals, his head gently oscillating. Then he turned to Moran with a look of grim determination on his face. 'Have you ever heard me speak of Sherlock Holmes?' he began. Moran's expression betrayed his interest. 'I see the name is not unfamiliar to you,'

Moriarty held up his hand. 'Let me finish. You should know that Holmes is a private detective, not long in the job, it's true, but already he has his finger very much on the pulse of criminal activity in London and beyond. He has made life difficult for me more than once in the past few years and I may have to take action, if he gets more persistent. He's already a force to be reckoned with.' Moriarty paused and shifted his position in the chair.

'He has, I'm told, moved to Baker Street. I need to know his exact address for obvious reasons and Slim has been given the job of finding it out. Hence his appearance there, but I'm surprised he wasn't a little more circumspect. Now you are fully in the picture.'

Moran was leaning forward in his chair, eager to tell what he knew. 'Look no further. Sherlock Holmes and I are both tenants in the same house in Baker Street. I'm in 221C and he's in 221B. We're on good terms already — I had sherry with him this morning.'

Moriarty leapt to his feet with a shout of joy. 'This is the best news yet. My chief of staff on social terms with Sherlock Holmes!' Moriarty glanced sharply at Moran, who was delighted at the impression his news had made on him. 'He doesn't know of your connection with me?'

'I can't see how that could be possible. We met for the first time only this morning and your name didn't come up in the conversation.'

Moriarty began to pace, obviously deep in thought, his head oscillating more than usual. 'Excellent,' he murmured, almost as though thinking aloud. 'We must take advantage of this close proximity to a man who could be dangerous to the organisation.'

Moran watched him, fascinated to see the master at work.

'We must make sure he never suspects that you are in any way connected with me,' went on Moriarty as he developed his thoughts. 'We must find some subtle means of feeding him false information through you about our projects, information we would like him to have to put him off the scent, when we are planning a major operation.'

Moran's face lit up at the thought of such a vital role for him to play. It could only enhance his status and put him in excellent standing with Moriarty.

'He already thinks I have criminal tendencies.'

'Does he really?' Moriarty stopped pacing and looked at Moran. 'How on earth could he know that after such a short acquaintance?'

'That was just one of a series of deductions he made when he first saw me. Some were a bit too close for comfort.'

'Right,' said Moriarty decisively,' That's the chink in his armour. We'll turn his deductive skills against himself.'

It was Moran's turn to look puzzled. 'How do you mean?'

'You could begin to play the role of a reformed character, trying hard to keep on the right side of the tracks at last. Your former colleagues, however, keep trying to involve you in their schemes and so you inform Holmes of exactly what they are to show him you have turned over a new leaf. He'll act on the information all right, only something will go wrong. He may also begin to doubt his own powers. The more I think of this the better I like it. The long-term effects could be catastrophic for Holmes.'

'A brilliant notion,' chortled Moran, 'I think I'll start the ball rolling right away, in case he's already got wind of our Swiss operation.'

'Now be careful,' warned Moriarty. 'Don't give too much away. Just enough false information for his agile brain to work on. He loves a challenge and should be left to ferret things out for himself.'

'Of course. Leave it to me. Just snippets I've picked up, plus inaccurate locations. I'll pay him another social call early next week just before I leave for Zurich. By the way, will we see you in Switzerland?'

'No, I'll stay here in case any problems arise. Slim will meet you over there. Remember, he has all the local knowledge and contacts. Make full use of him. I wish you the best of luck.'

The two men shook hands and Moran left the house.

* ★ *

Wet cobblestones gleaming in the moon-light, church steeples looming majestically into the starry sky on either bank of the river, lamp-lights flickering mysteriously in the misty air — memorable images they undoubtedly were, though they played no part in Moran's impressions of Zurich that Saturday night. His concentration on the serious job in hand was complete. He and Slim had arranged to meet Ben and Joe at an hour before midnight in the narrow alleyway behind the imposing *Loewen und Daumen* bank building in *Maehnestrasse*. Albert and Sam would join them later. They had a long night ahead of them.

Slim took out his pocket watch. 'They should be here at any moment.' Sure enough, Ben and Joe materialized out of the darkness exactly on time.

Moran nodded curtly. 'Did you bring all the equipment?'

'It's in the wagon. We left it tucked away round the corner as instructed. Fred has stayed on guard,' replied Ben.

'Better go and fetch it now,' growled Moran. 'And be quick about it; we've no time to dawdle.'

The two men ran off up the alley and disappeared into the darkness.

Slim looked up at the roof of the building, pointing out the huge, central chimney to Moran. 'It's a converted manor house, hence the chimney stacks. The middle one isn't used, however, and it gives direct access to the vaults. As Moriarty instructed, that's our way in tonight.'

'Moriarty worked out from the original plans of the building that it would be wide enough to allow Ben and Joe to climb down, but, looking at it, I'm not so sure.' Moran stroked his moustache.

'I've examined the chimney from the inside,' explained Slim, 'and I'm sure they can do it. They were chosen for this job precisely because of their slight builds.' As he spoke, the two men came back, staggering under the weight of several large boxes which they placed on the ground with sighs of relief.

Moran looked at each in turn. 'Now,

one of you has to go down first to deal with the guard. Remember what Moriarty told us: it's a special shipment of gold bars that we're after. They're being stored here for this weekend only before being transferred to a more secure location elsewhere, so we must expect them to be well guarded.'

'I'll go,' volunteered Ben, slipping a deadly looking knife into his belt.

'Whatever you have to do, make it silent,' advised Moran. 'We don't want the alarm to be raised.'

With a wave of his hand, Ben climbed over the wall and onto the roof before disappearing behind the chimney.

Moran turned to Slim. 'You have a technical briefing for these men, I know, so I'll leave you to it. I'll go round to the front of the building to make sure you're not disturbed.' He turned and walked back down the alley into the street.

The gas lamps cast vague, flickering shadows along the shop fronts, providing Moran with excellent cover, as he glided smoothly along past the main doors of the bank. He took up his position under a tree a little further on, so he would have as much warning as possible, if a policeman approached the bank. He looked along the street. Not a soul moved. A gentle stirring of leaves in the trees could be heard, as the breeze picked up a little. All at once another sound caught his ear, so faint at first that he thought he must have imagined it. Then it came again, louder this time, from further down the street. Moran crept to the end of the alleyway in case he had to run back and give the alarm to Slim and his men. Then he waited with bated breath.

The moon came out from behind a bank of clouds, bathing the whole street in an eerie glow. The tall figure of a man slowly emerged from the corner. He was wearing a uniform and pushing something in front of him. Moran heaved a sigh of relief. It was a street cleaner at work, making the most of the deserted streets to clean up before another day began.

Moran walked back along the alley to check what progress was being made. He looked up at the roof of the building and made out the forms of three men silhouetted against the night sky. 'Good,' he muttered. 'Ben must have dealt with the guard.' As he drew near, he could see the men were poring over a document. Moran realised it was Slim giving Ben and Joe their final briefing.

Slim had said he would go over just one more time the exact location of the hidden trip-wires strategically placed all round the gold bars. His detailed preparation and research were proving invaluable. Slim had managed to secure employment at this branch of the bank some months ago and the profitable use of his time there was paying dividends tonight. The way would soon be clear for the actual process of removing the gold bars to begin. Ben would go down to the vault again, this time with Joe. They would load the bars onto the hoist in batches of four, ready for Slim to pull them up the chimney.

A footstep crunched heavily on the gravel behind Moran.

He spun round quickly and was relieved to see the burly shapes of Albert and Sam, the remaining members of the gang. Their role would be a vital one: helping to carry the gold bars from the roof to the wagon ready for the getaway. Moran showed them the ladder they were to use. Without a word, they climbed up and joined their colleagues by the chimney stack. Satisfied that all was proceeding according to plan, Moran returned to the front of the building and took up his position again in the shadow of the tree. Glancing up at the roof, however, he noticed that the silhouettes of the men were clearly visible from the street. That could spell danger.

Moran returned to the back of the building, where he met Sam, who was just coming down with the first of the gold bars, neatly stacked in the hod he was carrying. He asked Sam to warn Slim and the others to keep on this side of the chimney as much as possible. As he was about to resume his vigil on the street, something made him stop. He listened hard.

Soon, he heard the slow, rhythmic tread of heavy boots along the pavement.

71

Moran pressed himself close to the wall and waited. The footsteps drew nearer. The imposing figure of a policeman was briefly silhouetted against the lamplight and then the sound of footsteps slowly receded down the street. Moran mopped his brow with his white handkerchief and replaced it in his sleeve. The danger was over for the time being. He took up his position again under the tree and prepared for a long wait.

At two o'clock in the morning Moran left his post and went back up the alley to relieve Slim at the top of the pulley. Slim's expression told him all was going well. They changed places in silence, Slim going down the ladder and disappearing into the darkness to take up his vigil. Moran's new position gave him his first clear view of what was going on down below thanks to the glow from the dark lantern on the floor of the vault. Ben was passing the bars to Joe, who placed them in the hoist four at a time and pulled hard on the rope to raise them up to the top of the chimney. Moran lifted them out and put them in one of the hods at his side, ready for Albert or Sam to carry down the ladder. The process was running smoothly and they were on track to clear the whole vault before daybreak.

Suddenly the hypnotic rhythm of the pulley was disturbed by a frantic scuffling down below. Ben appeared to be struggling with someone on the floor. The guard must have recovered and had taken him by surprise. Then the crack of a pistol shot rang out and both men fell backwards, cutting across several of the tripwires. Within seconds, the alarm bells began to peal.

'Quick, climb up here,' yelled Moran. 'Leave everything. We've got to get out, before it's too late.'

Down below he could just make out the motionless body of the guard with Ben stretched out across him. Joe was starting to haul himself up the chimney, when another shot rang out. With a shriek, he fell back into the vault, dragging the pulley and hoist down on top of him.

Moran jumped back, as the end of the rope flew into the air. He realized there was nothing he could do to save the men, so he ran along the roof, and slid down the ladder. As he reached the ground, he almost collided with Slim, who had come sprinting round the building at the din.

'What on earth happened?' he gasped.

'No time now. Let's get to the wagon and out of here quick.' Moran led the way down the alley to where Fred was waiting.

Moran and Slim fastened down the canvas top to conceal the stacks of gold bars and jumped in. Fred drove off at speed, urging the horses to a gallop and heading for their next destination, the smelting plant on the outskirts of the city.

'Did Albert and Sam get away?' asked Moran.

'Yes, I saw them running off as fast as they could,' replied Slim. 'What went on down there in the vault?'

The sound of the bells was receding in the distance as Moran shook his head at the thought of the disastrous events he had just witnessed. 'Difficult to be precise. It looked as if the guard regained consciousness. Ben tried to grapple with him and in the struggle the gun went off and both of them fell across the tripwires. Ben must have got the worst of it, because the guard shot Joe as he was climbing to safety. Two good men lost.'

'I can't believe things went wrong so quickly,' said Slim. He looked back at the precious load in the wagon. 'Well, at least we got most of the gold, so Moriarty won't be too upset.'

'We've still got to bring it through successfully,' Moran reminded him. 'It isn't over yet.' He turned to Fred. 'Is it far to the smelting works?'

'About fifteen minutes to go.' Fred cracked his whip at the horses.

Slim looked back at the way they had come. Dawn was breaking over the great city. 'A magnificent sight, but I'm glad to see the back of it just the same.'

Moran had his eyes fixed on the road ahead. 'I hope they're ready for us.'

'True, we are a little earlier than I told them we would be, but Moriarty pays over the odds for work like this, so I shouldn't think it matters what time we arrive.'

'We can trust them, then? There's a lot

of money at stake here.'

'Moriarty has used this firm for many years and they've never let him down yet.'

Reassured, Moran stroked his moustache and settled down in silence for the rest of the journey.

Later, Slim interrupted Moran's musings. 'Look there, through the trees. Your first glimpse of the smelting plant. Not very romantic, is it?'

It certainly wasn't. A long, low brick structure with three enormous chimneys appeared in front of them. They pulled up at the main entrance as two uniformed officials ran out to greet them. Slim introduced Moran and Fred and they all went in together, while other uniformed men led the horses to a side entrance adapted to accommodate large delivery wagons.

Moran, Slim and Fred were shown into a spacious dining hall, where they were served a most welcome breakfast, after which they were escorted to a comfortable lounge to await the completion of the smelting. All three were exhausted after the events of the night and it wasn't long before they were stretched out, dozing in comfortable armchairs.

Slim was the first to wake and he went round to the office to check on progress. He was assured there were no problems in carrying out the special instructions for this particular job, but it would be another hour before all would be ready for collection.

Moran woke up a short time later. He looked around the strange surroundings, taking a little time to get his bearings. He stood, roused Fred from his slumbers, and turned to Slim. 'Are you sure they'll be able to carry out Moriarty's instructions. They were very unusual.'

'They always have. Why should this time be any different?'

'Maybe they haven't enough of the right moulds.'

'You worry too much. I've just checked and all is well.' As Slim spoke, one of the assistants came over to inform them that the finished product was ready for their inspection. Slim thanked the assistant, who then led the way through a side door into the vast finishing room.

What a strange sight met their eyes: arranged in serried ranks along the whole length of the room were hundreds of grey garden gnomes in a variety of shapes and sizes. Despite knowing what to expect, the three men gazed in amazement.

Moran was the first to react. 'Remarkable achievement. You have to hand it to Moriarty. How he thought up the idea, goodness knows.' He went over and picked up a figure of an old, gnarled gnome leaning on a garden spade. He held it up to his face and examined it closely. 'Exactly like an ordinary garden gnome. I'm stunned at the craftsmanship.'

Slim nodded his agreement. 'Who would think you're looking at hundreds of pounds worth of garden decoration under that grey exterior. We'll have no difficulty at all in exporting them to England.' He ran his fingers over a group of gnomes leapfrogging over each other.

The assistant was beaming with pleasure at so much praise. 'Glad you're pleased with them. Shall we pack them in their boxes and load them onto the wagon?'

'Yes, the sooner the better,' replied Moran.

'It's time we got started for home.'

'I assume Moriarty has already arranged for payment?' asked Slim.

'Indeed, sir, in the usual way,' replied the assistant. 'All is completely in order.'

'I left two large destination boards for the wagon and smaller ones for each box. Could you make sure they're fixed on securely, please?' asked Moran.

'Certainly, sir, it shall be done,' came the reply.

'Good. Let us know when all is ready.'

The three men had time for a last cup of coffee and then went outside to watch the final preparations. The destination boards had already been put in place. They read in large, black letters:

GARY DEBBS GARDEN SUPPLIES &
EQUIPMENT
MAIN DEPOT, RYBURN
SURREY, ENGLAND

Slim looked puzzled, when he read the name and address and turned to Moran. 'Who is this Gary Debbs? I've never heard of him.'

79

Moran laughed. 'I'm not surprised. He doesn't exist. It's a name Moriarty uses on collection points to store materials for future use. Our particular consignment will stay in this depot, until it's been checked by his experts, after which it will be smelted into gold bars again.'

The horses had already been harnessed, so Fred took his place in the driver's seat. Moran walked round the wagon, checking that all the crates were securely sealed and stored. He and Slim then shook hands with the smelting team, who had gathered to say farewell, and climbed onto the wagon. It was time to move off, on the long journey home. Moran had decided it would be safer to drive across the border and board a train at a French station.

After a few hours they arrived at the sleepy little town of Goumois in the Jura, and found themselves in France without any trouble at all. Moving on to Besancon, Moran made arrangements to have the crates loaded onto a goods train bound first for Paris and then the coast. The wagon and horses were then sold to a local dealer. A few hours later, they were on their way in one of the goods wagons, guarding the crates and enjoying a little more comfort than before. The rest of the journey to England passed off without incident and the crates were delivered safely to the depot at Ryburn. Moran left Slim to handle the paperwork at reception and took a cab to Moriarty's to give him a full report, dropping Fred off at his home on the way.

★ ★ ★

'Two men presumed dead and only part of the gold removed. Hardly the report I'd been expecting,' snapped Moriarty, pacing up and down in front of a fire in his lounge, his head oscillating rapidly.

'But — '

'No *buts*. I don't want excuses. I want results and if you can't deliver them, I'll have to find someone reliable who will.' Moriarty spun round and glared at Moran. 'Did you drop off whatever gold you managed to get at the depot?'

'Yes, we called in on the way here. I left

Slim supervising the transfer, while I came to make my report.' He opened the bag he was carrying. 'I thought you might like this as a souvenir.' He pulled out a small grey gnome and handed it to Moriarty.

'Ah, thank you. Nice to see what they actually look like. That consignment, small though it is, will serve to prop up our depleted coffers until we can manage a more profitable coup.'

He paused for a moment, looking down at the little gnome. His eyes glinted. 'Let's see, if you're worth your weight in gold.' He took out a small knife from his pocket and began to scrape at the lead surface. It seemed to have no effect. Moriarty frowned and scraped harder, then harder still as it became obvious that there was no gold at all beneath the lead surface.

The gnome was made entirely of lead.

Moriarty staggered back, dropping his knife. 'What's this!' He hurled the gnome across the room. 'You fool. You've been duped. You've just hauled a ton of lead half way across Europe. What happened to the gold?'

Moran's tan turned a shade lighter, as he reeled under Moriarty's fury. 'Perhaps this one got through in error,' he stammered.

'You'd better be right! Get back to the depot and check on the whole consignment.'

'I'm on my way,' gulped Moran, departing hastily.

★ ★ ★

There was a knock on the door of 221B Baker Street. Watson opened it to find a vaguely familiar figure on the doorstep.

'Could I have a word with Sherlock Holmes, please?'

Watson looked him up and down. What he saw did not impress him: a portly middle-aged man with a grizzled moustache and rather dilapidated clothing. However Watson was becoming accustomed to the varied clientele that Holmes entertained in the apartment, so he admitted the stranger.

'Mr Holmes is not here at the moment, but I'm expecting him presently, Mr . . . '

'Slim, just call me Slim. Mr Holmes will know who it is.'

'Well, if you don't mind waiting . . . sit down over here.' Watson indicated an armchair by the fire and went over to the table to continue his task of pasting newspaper articles into a large scrapbook.

'I must say it's good to be home again,' rang out a familiar voice.

Watson jumped up from the table. 'Holmes! What on earth — '

Holmes burst out laughing at the expression on Watson's face. 'You really will have to get used to my little disguises.' He pointed to the thinning grey wig, the grizzled moustache, and heavy padding that lay on the carpet. 'This one has proved invaluable. It's a real story for your archives too,' he added, stretching his arms above his head. 'Appearing to take several inches off my height is a trick I learnt in my early days of crime investigation. That, plus a few basic elements of disguise have always been effective,' he explained, painfully removing strips of rubber padding from inside his cheeks.

84

'The weight of all that padding was almost too much for me at times, but it was worth it for the insight it gave me into the detailed running of Moriarty's criminal empire.' He walked over to the side-table, where he washed his hands and face in a bowl of hot water, before creaming himself thoroughly to remove the last vestiges of make-up.

Watson had recovered his composure. 'Thank you for all those telegrams, Holmes,' he said, handing him a towel. 'They certainly helped me keep track of your activities.'

'Glad they reached you safely. They gave you a rough outline of what I was up to, but now I'm in a position to provide some titbits to whet your appetite.' He finished drying himself and pulled up a chair. 'I had the real Slim arrested the moment he set foot on Swiss soil. He had all the details of the Zurich bank and the arrangements for disposing of the gold on him. He is now languishing in a Swiss prison, with a history of violent crime behind him. I took his place just before Moran arrived in Zurich.'

Watson looked puzzled. 'But what I don't understand is how you found out that Moriarty was planning a raid on a bank in Zurich in the first place. I accept you have wonderful powers of deduction, but that's going a little far, even for you.'

'Ah, I cheated there, I'm afraid. You remember I looked after Moran's valise, while he chased after Slim? Well, a quick glance at the papers in the case told me all I needed — that, plus what Moran didn't tell me in that second conversation we had.'

'So, you've been with Moran all this time and he suspected nothing?'

'Not a thing. He was so absorbed in what he was doing that he had little time for me.'

Holmes paused for a moment, his brow furrowed. 'That wasn't so with Ben and Joe, I'm sorry to say. They had worked closely with the real Slim in the past and were beginning to suspect something. That led to my one regret: having to fire my pistol at Joe, though I hope I only wounded him.'

'How did that come about?' asked Watson.

Holmes went on slowly. 'I had to try to stop the robbery or at least cut down the amount of gold they actually stole, so I got into the vault by a side entrance and was just in time to see the guard struggling with Ben. They fell across the tripwires and set off the bells. When the guard's gun went off and Ben collapsed, Joe tried to escape up the chimney shaft. He had seen me in the vault and I couldn't let him climb up and give me away.' He sighed, stood up, went over to the corner where he had left his bag, and delved into it. He pulled out two little grey garden gnomes and held them up for Watson. 'Souvenirs of my trip. They'll look good on our mantelshelf.'

'Why garden gnomes?' asked Watson. 'I don't see the point.'

'The idea was to turn the gold bars into innocent-looking gnomes for easy transport into England, where they would revert to their natural state. Amazing what a little — er — pecuniary inducement will do to change a man's mind. The owner of the plant simply supplied Moran with a whole consignment of lead garden gnomes, a standard shipment regularly exported to England and elsewhere. I had the gold bars sent straight back to the bank, where they came from. That's why Moran had such a trouble-free journey home.'

'A most ingenious ending to a great adventure,' said Watson. 'It will need very few of those extra embellishments that you're always telling me I spoil my narratives with.'

'None at all, I hope, except perhaps a pithy account of Moriarty's reaction, when he learns the whole truth about his venture,' replied Holmes. 'That, I look forward to reading.'

The Disappearance of Lord Lexingham

It was with a deep sense of foreboding that Moran went back to his apartment at 221C Baker Street the day after the disastrous Zurich affair. He had left the previous week well aware that he had a potentially dangerous foe living on the floor above, but only now did he realize just how dangerous Sherlock Holmes could be. Moriarty had immediately suspected Holmes' involvement once he learned of Slim's imprisonment and the total loss of the gold. His fury over Holmes successful deception knew no bounds. It was even greater than when Moran had reported that the whole consignment in the depot was in fact made of lead. The humiliation of being so thoroughly outwitted by Holmes was just too much.

Moran was still smarting from the harsh criticism levelled at him by Moriarty, as he made his way down the stairs to the apartment. He would have to change his lodgings, of course, but Moriarty had asked him to postpone this for the time being, a request that Moran found difficult to understand. Now that his involvement with Moriarty was known to Holmes, there was surely no longer any advantage in living in such close proximity. No doubt Moriarty had his reasons, which he would explain in his own good time. That would probably have to wait, however, until after the next major project, which Moriarty was eager to begin right away. From what he had said, it would be more ambitious in scope than anything he had attempted before and Moran would be fully involved for weeks to come. Details were to be given at a meeting to be held the next day.

★   ★   ★

'Any questions?' Moriarty's voice boomed out across the room. The twelve men sitting at the table in Moriarty's lounge skimmed through the notes they'd been taking during the meeting. One or two raised their hands to have points of detail clarified, but in general they all seemed satisfied with Moriarty's presentation.

Like the others, Moran had listened attentively. Now he leaned forward, stroking his moustache thoughtfully. 'Just two points, Professor. How will our operatives get close enough to their targets to be effective?'

'They are already in positions of trust with the selected families.' Six of the heads around the table nodded in agreement.

Moran sat back in his chair, aware for the first time of the real depths of Moriarty's criminal ingenuity. Moriarty must have been planning this project over a very long period of time, as the operatives must have been placed in the families months — even years — before to be in such intimate contact with them now.

'Your second point?' Moriarty's voice brought him back sharply to the matter in hand.

Moran cleared his throat. 'Our last project was equally well organized, but it didn't turn out to be effective once

Holmes got wind of it. What are your plans to make sure this doesn't happen again?'

Moriarty controlled himself with a great effort, and managed a sardonic smile.

'You can well imagine that I've given that a lot of thought. We can't afford to be caught out twice.' His eyes flashed, as he looked witheringly at Moran. 'You'll be pleased to hear that my plans are foolproof this time. Not even Mr Sherlock Holmes will be able to penetrate them.' Moriarty banged his fists on the tabletop. 'I'm taking no chances and — to make doubly sure nothing goes wrong — I've assigned you a special role, Moran. I want you to take advantage of your proximity to Holmes to keep a close watch on all his movements. That must be your priority. I'll tell you when to make your move against your allocated target in the main scheme of things. It will obviously be later than the others, but no matter.' He looked down at his papers and made some notes. 'Yours will be the last one, in fact.'

Moran's face expressed his disappointment. 'I had hoped for a more prestigious assignment. Postponing my main task just to follow Holmes about hardly seems the best use of my talents.'

Moriarty glared at him. 'It's a vital role and you've been chosen because you are the one most suited to carry it out well.'

Moran was somewhat mollified by these comments.

'If you'd waited a moment, you'd have learnt that I've saved the most dramatic assignment for you,' added Moriarty. 'Details will come later, but it will take place after all the others have been completed. Jack and his team will work with you on this occasion.'

A lone head nodded on the far side of the table. Moran pulled at his moustache, satisfied at his revised role.

Moriarty paused for a moment and then addressed the rest of the group. 'Remember, contact your appropriate domestic staff only when your initial assignment has been completed satisfactorily. That will be their signal to act. Finally, there must be no communication whatsoever with me after today, until the whole project is finished.' He tidied his papers, wished his men good luck, and left the room.

* * *

The month after the Zurich affair proved an unusually busy one for Holmes and Watson. The international ramifications of a double murder case that had baffled Scotland Yard absorbed a great deal of their time. Other less important, but nevertheless interesting cases filled the rest of the month and provided Holmes with the intellectual stimulation he so craved. They also gave Watson the opportunity to bring Holmes' name to the attention of the public for the first time through a series of articles in the press. In fact, it was early April before Holmes was once again beginning to complain about the lamentable lack of criminal activity in London. When these moods of depression came over him, they revealed a different side to his character, one that gave Watson no pleasure at all.

It was therefore with eager anticipation that Watson went to the door one morning in answer to Mrs Hudson's gentle tapping. She held out her silver salver and her lips curved into a hint of a smile when Watson picked up the visiting card.

'Lady Lexingham,' he said loudly, so that Holmes would hear. 'Would you ask Her Ladyship if she would be so good as to come up, please, Mrs Hudson?'

A few moments later a beautiful young woman attired in a silk dress of apple green stood upon the threshold. 'Mr Sherlock Holmes?' she asked in a delicate, clear voice.

'My name is Watson, Your Ladyship, Dr Watson. This is Mr Holmes.' He stood aside to present Holmes.

On hearing the name of their distinguished visitor, Holmes had risen from the table where he had been conducting his chemical experiments and come over to the door.

'Good morning, Your Ladyship. I am Sherlock Holmes. Please come in and take a chair.'

The young lady came in a little

hesitantly, but appeared relieved at the warmth of her reception. Her dress rustled as she sat down.

'Now,' began Holmes, sitting opposite her and leaning forward, his elbows firmly planted on his knees and his chin resting in his hands. 'How can I be of assistance?'

'I'll come straight to the point, Mr Holmes. I'm at my wits' end and I don't know which way to turn.' Her voice broke for a moment and then, with an effort, she controlled herself again. 'My husband is normally a man of regular habits, but lately he has taken to walking in his sleep — not just inside the house, but outside in the grounds too. When he opens the door, I can clearly hear a sustained high-pitched whistle coming from some-where on the estate. I've no idea where he goes, but on his return, his face and hands are covered in soil. He remembers nothing of this when he wakes up.' She took a dainty muslin handkerchief from her handbag and dabbed her eyes. 'Two nights ago he went out and has not returned since. I need your help to find out what's happened to him, Mr Holmes.'

Holmes pursed his thin lips. 'You say this began lately. Did you notice anything unusual that could account for the remarkable change in your husband's behaviour?'

'Yes. Last week a letter arrived for him and he seemed disturbed by the contents. I found this envelope in his desk this morning and brought it with me.' She opened her handbag and handed a buff-coloured envelope to Holmes.

Inside was a sheet of white writing paper, blank except for a charcoal drawing of a black lacquered oblong box inside a blue circle. Holmes passed the paper over to Watson. 'I must admit this drawing means nothing to me at the moment, but I will certainly take up the case and try to find out all I can.'

'I've brought a small portrait he had done last year, so you can see what he looks like.' Lady Lexingham gave Holmes a picture of a tall, handsome young man in evening dress.

Holmes looked at it carefully. 'Thank you.' He handed it to Watson. 'That will be very useful indeed. It would also help me if we could come and visit you as soon as possible to look round the house and grounds.'

'Of course. The address is Beechcroft Manor, Reibridge, Surrey. I'll expect you tomorrow after lunch, if that suits your plans.' She stood and smiled gratefully at Holmes.

'We shall be there.' Holmes escorted her to the door. 'Goodbye, madam, until tomorrow.' He closed the door and leaned his back against it. 'Most intriguing. What do you make of her, Watson?'

'A remarkably attractive woman,' was the reply.

'Was she? I didn't notice. I was examining what she was wearing. Did you notice she had on a Paisley shawl, when I would have expected Cashmere from a lady of her standing? Her gloves were short — last year's fashion, in fact — and noticeably worn around the finger tips. Her shoes had been soled. There were other minor points of interest about her, but those were the most pertinent.'

Watson bent forward in his chair, impressed with his companion's keen powers of observation. 'And what do you deduce from all that, may I ask?'

'The family is no longer as affluent as it once was. That may have no bearing at all on the case in hand, but it's important to be aware of such matters. However, let's postpone judgement until after our visit tomorrow.'

Holmes walked over to a small side-table, pulled up a chair and began to examine the drawing on the paper. 'Come over here, Watson, and let's see, what we can make of this.'

Watson joined him at the table and studied the paper carefully. 'A symbol of some kind, obviously. Perhaps the circle denotes a certain degree of exclusivity — perhaps the box is a limited edition?'

'But why a box in the first place and a lacquered one at that?' said Holmes. 'The contrast between the rectangular lines and the circle offers distinct possibilities, however. The box could be bursting to reveal its secrets and the ring restricting access to a select few. Hmm.' He pushed the paper aside. 'We need a little more information before we begin to draw conclusions. Let's put it out of our minds until after our visit. Meanwhile we have just a short time to wait before Mrs Hudson is due to send up our luncheon.'

Leaving the paper on the table, Holmes crossed the room, took out his violin from its case and began to play a plaintive, soothing melody. Watson smiled, produced his pen and notebook, and began work on his diary of the case so far.

★   ★   ★

Following Holmes had seemed an easy option to Moran, when Moriarty had announced it at the meeting a few weeks ago, but he had reckoned without the detective's abundant energy. Holmes seemed to have covered half of London over the past month and it was proving a punishing schedule for Moran. He would have preferred to be getting on with his main task, like the rest of his colleagues, who were now well advanced with their work. Some had already reached the second stage and made contact with the appropriate domestic staff as instructed. Moran had been glad, therefore, to note a distinct slackening in Holmes' activity of late. He knew it couldn't last, of course, and — sure enough — one afternoon in April the door of the apartment above banged to and two pairs of shoes pounded rapidly down the stairs.

The chase had begun again.

Moran was lucky enough to find a cab shortly after Holmes and Watson disappeared round the corner in theirs, and he instructed the driver to follow at a discreet distance. It was quite a journey to Beechcroft Manor, but eventually Holmes and Watson's cab turned into Lord Lexingham's estate. Moran dismissed his cab a few yards back along the road and walked the rest of the way.

★   ★   ★

Holmes handed his card to the footman, and he and Watson were quickly shown into an elegantly-appointed drawing room. A gentle rustling was distinctly audible from the corridor, before Lady Lexingham appeared to greet her visitors. The royal blue of her gown complemented the gold and silver trimmings of the sumptuous furnishings.

'I'm so glad you were able to come, gentlemen. I have some new information for you.'

She opened a drawer in the bureau by the fireplace, took out a piece of writing paper, and handed it to Holmes. It was a sheet of printed stationery with a picture of the familiar lacquered box inside a blue circle in the top right-hand corner. This time, however, the letters 'K.I.S.' were printed in large bold letters just below the picture.

'Yes, this does give us something more to go on,' said Holmes, studying the paper carefully. 'Did His Lordship ever receive letters from a company using these letters?'

'No, not to my knowledge.'

'Would you mind, if I took this away with me to study more closely?'

'Of course not. Is there anything else I can do to assist you?'

'If I could be permitted to stroll round the grounds to see where His Lordship's perambulations took him?'

'Certainly. Oh, Mr Holmes, use all your skills, I beg you! There must be some evidence out there to indicate what might have happened to him.' She dabbed her eyes with an embroidered silk hand-kerchief, touched a bell-pull near the curtains, and a footman appeared to escort Holmes and Watson.

'Try not to worry too much. If I discover anything of real importance, I'll let you know right away,' said Holmes. When he reached the door, he glanced back into the room. Lady Lexingham had sunk down into a chair, her head slumped forward, the very picture of dejection.

Holmes lost no time in beginning his investigations. As soon as he emerged from the house, he whipped out his magnifying glass, threw himself to the ground, and proceeded to crawl along the path at the edge of the garden. When he came to a small shed at the end of the path, he leapt to his feet, examined the latch carefully, and went inside. Watson followed. Garden tools hung on the walls and seed trays were stacked in orderly fashion. Holmes did not waste time on them. His attention was drawn to a huge mound of soil completely filling the far end of the shed. A large garden spade stuck out of it at an angle. Holmes grabbed it and dug deep into the soil in various places. Finally he put the spade down and turned to Watson.

'We've drawn a blank, it would appear. Footprints I take to be Lord Lexingham's lead right up to the shed, but none return. There's no way out except the way we came in, yet we know he regularly went back to the house after his perambulations. On the face of it, then, we have an impossible situation.'

Watson was looking hard at the pile of soil. 'How did he get covered in this stuff? What was he trying to do?'

'Bury or search for something, I suppose,' replied Holmes. 'But,' his voice dropped to a whisper, 'what if there was another reason?' He struck his forehead with the palm of his hand. 'Of course! What a dolt I've been not to think of this before. We ought to have looked outside the shed. Come along Watson. We're on to something here.'

Meanwhile, Moran had edged closer when he saw the men enter the shed. He disappeared behind a convenient bush when the door creaked open again. He watched them emerge and go round to the back of the shed, where they both poked around the undergrowth concealing the panels. After a short while, one large panel swung loose on well-oiled hinges, releasing a substantial shower of soil onto the ground.

'So,' exclaimed Holmes, 'this was his escape route, deep down under the pile of soil. There must be a side entrance to the house nearby.'

Watson walked up to the house and called back to Holmes. 'There's a door here, leading to the kitchen.'

Holmes came up to join him and looked satisfied. 'I think we've done all we can here this afternoon, Watson. It's back to Baker Street for us now to see what we can make of the information available to us.'

Moran looked on as Holmes and

Watson walked down the long drive to the main gate. Then he made his way back to report to Moriarty on the afternoon's activities.

⋆ ⋆ ⋆

Back in Baker Street, Holmes lost no time in trying to interpret the picture and letters on the printed stationery. 'The K could stand for *kreis*, the German word for circle,' he murmured as he and Watson sat at table, surrounded by reference books.

Watson flicked open a book on industries located in and around London. 'There is a firm called 'Kreis Industries Limited' listed. It's a manufacturing company and could make boxes,' he said.

'Let me have a look,' said Holmes. 'Hmm. Yes, you may be right. It's certainly worth following up. Where's the head office?'

'In the Mile End Road.'

'That should round off our day very nicely, but first we need some refreshment, don't you think? Would you ask Mrs Hudson, if she would send up some

106

of those tasty ham sandwiches she does so well, please? We'll have plenty of time to pay a visit to Kreis Industries before they close.'

On his way back upstairs, Watson picked up a copy of the *Star*, which was lying on the hall table, and glanced at the headlines while he waited for afternoon tea. He didn't get further than page one. 'I say, Holmes, this may be of interest to you. It says here that over the past week six prominent businessmen living in or around London have been found dead in their homes. Cause of death unknown. Scotland Yard has been called in to investigate. Names and addresses are all provided, if you would care to see them.'

Holmes lit his favourite cherrywood pipe. Only a slight twitch of the eyebrows showed that he had heard what Watson had said. 'That's hardly headline material. The verdict will probably turn out to be death from natural causes, like the large number of deaths that go unreported week after week in the London area. It's a wonder that the foul London air we breathe and the stench of the filth in our streets don't send a lot more of us to an early grave. Ah, here comes Mrs Hudson with the tea and sandwiches.'

The efforts of the afternoon had indeed given both men a keen appetite and Mrs Hudson had excelled herself. They were not to have the opportunity to enjoy the meal in peace, however, for no sooner had Watson poured himself a second cup of tea, than there was a loud knock on the door. Inspector Lestrade strode in without further ceremony.

'Ah, do come in, Lestrade. Have a sandwich. They're delicious,' said Holmes.

'No time, I'm afraid. Apologies for the intrusion, by the way, but I was too busy to call ahead.' He collapsed into a chair by the fire.

'So I observe,' remarked Holmes.

'I need your help urgently!'

'Oh, you mean that business of the mysterious deaths of the six business-men?' Holmes raised his cup to his lips.

'How did you know — ' Lestrade caught sight of Watson holding up the newspaper. 'Ah. I've nothing to go on, you see. All six deaths were apparently from natural causes.'

Holmes cast a meaningful glance at Watson. 'But for me, that's too much of a coincidence over such a short period of time. I'm making no progress, however, Mr Holmes and I thought maybe — '

Holmes shook his head. 'I'm sorry, Lestrade, but I'm extremely busy at the moment. Watson and I are about to leave in fact.'

Lestrade's face fell. 'I was relying on you, Holmes.'

Holmes put down his cup and saucer, and escorted Lestrade to the door. 'It's just not possible at present, as I've explained. If, however, you haven't solved the case — assuming, of course, that there is a case — by next week, then I should be happy to assist you as best I can. Good afternoon.'

Lestrade looked even more downcast, but there was nothing to be done.

Holmes closed the door quietly. 'Time we left for Kreis Industries, Watson.'

Within a few minutes the two men were sitting in a cab heading for the Mile End Road. Unknown to them another cab had set off behind them with a familiar figure on board. It didn't take long for Holmes to realize his mistake once he and Watson entered the imposing edifice of Kreis Industries. Pictures of enormous steel structures displayed across all the walls in the vast entrance hall clearly showed that the firm's main manufacturing interests did not lie in the production of tiny lacquered boxes. A brief conversation with the sales manager revealed that they did not use the picture of a box in a circle on their printed stationery either and had no idea who did. Disappointed, Holmes and Watson set off for home. Once again, they were followed at a discreet distance.

Holmes was not in a talkative mood and Watson failed to rouse him from his gloom with his well-intentioned comments on the passing scenes. One comment, however, had an effect. Watson had mentioned the cab behind them, which was repeatedly reflected in shop windows as they passed.

Holmes glanced back, and then addressed the cabbie. 'Take us home the long way, would you? The scenic route!' He laughed heartily. 'Let's give him a run for his money, shall we? See if you can make out who it is, Watson.' In no time at all, they were heading for the Tower of London, where Holmes asked the driver to slow down, so he could appreciate the full splendour of the ancient fortress.

Watson took the chance to get a closer look at the cab behind, as the gap between them narrowed.

'He sports a glorious moustache, whoever he is. I've a feeling we've seen it before.'

'Moran! What the deuce is he doing following us around? Moriarty's up to no good if he's so keen to keep a check on my whereabouts.'

The cab entered Parliament Square, where Holmes expressed a keen interest in the Houses of Parliament and had the cabbie move at a snail's pace as they passed. 'Shall we drop in on the Grand Old Man, do you think? No, perhaps not. He's enough on his plate at the moment. All right, driver, back to Baker Street. That's enough to give Moran food for thought, eh, Watson? I wonder what Moriarty will make of that.'

On his return to Baker Street, Holmes consulted his reference books once more. Well, we've examined the circle. What about the box itself?' Holmes quickly looked up 'lacquered boxes' in a large illustrated tome. 'What a fool I've been, Watson! Here's a firm that specializes in lacquered boxes.' He pointed to a drawing very similar to the one they had. 'Kiiroashi, a town near Tokyo seems to be the world-wide centre for the production of decorative, lacquered boxes and cabinets. And, look here, there's a mention of Kiiroashi Industries Limited having its main London office in the Old Kent Road. We've got our destination for tomorrow!' He snapped the book closed with a flourish.

'It does sound much more hopeful,' agreed Watson, putting the volumes back on the shelves.

'That's all we can do for this evening,' said Holmes, leaning back in his chair and stretching out his legs. 'What do you think about treating ourselves to a meal at Simpson's? I've reserved a box for us at eight. We deserve a little cheering up after the events of the day, I think.'

★ ★ ★

The next morning saw Holmes and Watson at the main office of Kiiroashi Industries in conversation with the sales manager. At first it seemed they were once again on the wrong track. The firm did not use the box and circle symbol on their printed stationery. The sales manager went on to say that their subsidiary, Kiiroashi Insurance Limited, did use a similar motif, however. It might be worth while visiting them. As it happened, their main office was situated on the seventh floor of the same building.

Holmes thanked the manager, then he and Watson made their way upstairs. 'Kiiroashi Insurance — of course. That's far more likely to have been the subject of correspondence with Lord Lexingham than an industrial firm. I should have thought of that earlier. It would have saved us so much time.'

Holmes and Watson waited in the reception room, and it wasn't long before the accounts manager came out to greet them. Holmes explained who they were and what they were trying to do as succinctly as possible and produced the sheet of printed stationery.

'Yes,' said the accounts manager, giving it a cursory glance. 'That is a sheet of our stationery. That is our particular symbol.'

'Excellent,' replied Holmes. 'This paper was found in Lord Lexingham's desk and it would be of great help to me, if you could let me know whether he took out a life insurance policy with your firm over the past few weeks.'

'We never reveal the names of our clients, I'm afraid,' replied the manager.

'This is not a frivolous enquiry. It could be a matter of life or death and — if the latter — the name of the beneficiary of such a policy could be of vital importance to me and to the police.'

The manager hesitated for a moment, pursed his lips, and then said he would have to consult the general manager. He excused himself and left the room via a door at the rear.

Holmes shook his head in impatience and had just opened his mouth to speak to Watson, when the man reappeared, carrying a huge black ledger.

'You're extremely fortunate. The general manager is aware of the value of your work, Mr Holmes, and has instructed me to provide you with every assistance.'

Holmes couldn't resist a quick glance at Watson, who bowed his head and gave a wry smile.

The manager placed the ledger on a large desk in the centre of the room, opened it at a page containing a long list of names and addresses, and stepped away to give Holmes room to work. 'All these gentlemen took out life insurance policies with this company over the past few weeks.'

Holmes' long finger ran down the list, then he looked up, disappointment written all over his lean features. 'There's no mention of Lord Lexingham's name here. I thought I was close to a solution, but once again it was not to be.'

Watson's eyes were still fixed on the page. 'You're right about that, Holmes, there's no such name here, but there is something that might be significant.'

'What are you talking about?'

'Look at this, Holmes,' he whispered. 'The last six names on the list are the same as the ones I read in today's *Star*. The names of the men who died over the past week.'

Holmes examined the list again. 'Are you sure?'

'Yes.'

'May we have a copy of this list, please?' asked Holmes.

'Of course,' replied the accounts manager.

'Watson, your powers of observation do you credit.' Holmes clapped Watson on the shoulder. 'It seems Lestrade may indeed have a case, and a serious one at that.' Watson's face showed his pleasure at the compliment, for praise from that quarter was rare. The accounts manager handed a copy of the list to Holmes, who thanked him for his cooperation and asked to be informed if there should be any additions made to the list in the future. Then he and Watson left the building and took a cab back to Baker Street. 'If Moran is still following us, let him get on with it. This is too important for us to be bothered with extraneous matters.' He spent the rest of the journey deep in thought, hardly noticing when they arrived in Baker Street.

Watson lost no time in checking the names with the list in the *Star*: they were identical.

Holmes nodded. 'I never had any doubt.' He curled up in his favourite armchair, and lit his cherrywood pipe with a taper from the embers of the fire. 'Would you mind, if I set out my thoughts on what we learnt this morning, old fellow? I feel it would help to disperse a little of the fog that still hangs over this murky business.'

'I'd be delighted,' replied Watson, pulling his chair closer to the fire.

'Well, we may have come to a dead end for the moment in our search for Lord Lexingham, but I fancy the trail has inadvertently led us to what could be a crime of monstrous proportions — multiple murder, no less.'

Watson's jaw dropped. 'You deduced that from examining the list in the ledger?'

Holmes shook his head vigorously. 'No, *you* did. Without your noticing the similarity between the two lists I would have drawn no conclusions at all. Now it is a list of dead men.' He pulled out the copy of the list from his pocket. 'Look at the dates on which these insurance policies were taken out. They were all within a week of each other. Considered as isolated cases, they could be put down as mere coincidence, but, when compared with the same list from the *Star*, a different picture with a far more sinister aspect emerges. All six men died within a few weeks of taking out the policies.'

'That would indeed be stretching coincidence too far, but why would anyone contrive to bring about the deaths of these six men?'

'Indeed,' agreed Holmes, knocking out his pipe on the grate. 'But there you have hit upon the one missing element that would link all these deaths together and unravel the mystery: motive. To establish that, we have to know the names of the beneficiaries of all the policies and for that we're going to need official police help. The company is very unlikely to provide us with unlimited access to their records, especially once they realise that they may be implicated.'

'That may take some time,' said Watson. He paused for a moment, his brow furrowed. 'A visit to the Registrar's office is called for, I think. My medical knowledge should help me assess the causes of the deaths. Shall I go right away?'

Holmes nodded his agreement. Watson picked up his coat and hat and left the room. As he went out, he passed Lestrade going in, looking as worried as before.

'Holmes, I've come back, because I'm still at a loss. If ever I needed your help, it's now.'

'*Nil desperandum*, Lestrade.' Holmes rose from his chair and handed him the list of names from the insurance company. He quickly brought him up-to-date on all the information he had obtained.

'Remarkable, Holmes, remarkable. And to think these are the results you get when you are not working on a case!' Lestrade shook his head in disbelief.

'Watson has gone off to the Registrar's to try to find the exact causes of death.'

'He'll draw a blank, I'm afraid. *Natural*

causes appears on the records. What were you expecting him to find?'

'An indication, however vague, of something unusual in the details of the cases. I'm convinced there's more to it than you think.'

'So it would seem from what you've already discovered. I'm not convinced by the coincidence theory, either, but where's the proof, Holmes? Highly suspicious the circumstances may be, but suspicion won't bring a successful court case. A British jury needs hard evidence that a crime has been committed. We can't go round arresting everyone who has benefitted from a life insurance policy.'

'I'm well aware of all that, but my instincts tell me I'm right. These deaths simply cannot be as innocent as they are made out to be.'

'Well, let's have your theory, then. You're a marvellous one for theorizing, I know, but bear in mind that a theory is all it can be at this stage.'

'I believe the six beneficiaries were working together as a group, following a carefully prepared plan which was designed to speed up the process of dying quite considerably.'

'A conspiracy, eh? Holmes, that's going a bit too far even for you. Where's the evidence?'

'Only the unusually close proximity of dates in the signing of the policies and the deaths of the policy holders. At least it's a working hypothesis in the absence of anything else.'

'I'm intrigued to hear how this concerted plan could possibly speed up the process so precisely in each case.'

'Poisoning. The slow, methodical, calculated poisoning of each man concerned.'

'That's too fantastic, Holmes. There would be clear traces evident in the autopsies.'

'Not if arsenic was used. It leaves no trace in the bloodstream, as you are no doubt aware.'

Lestrade appeared to be impressed and fell silent for a moment. 'It's true that statistics show that arsenic poisoning is the most frequent method of committing murder, but to find it being used on this scale would be unprecedented, if proved. What do we know about the beneficiaries?' he asked.

121

'Nothing. That's where I shall need your help. Only official police action will prise that kind of information from the insurance company.'

'Consider it done, Holmes,' Lestrade replied enthusiastically.

Holmes stood. 'Excellent. We oughtn't to waste another moment. Can you spare the time now?'

'Of course. I want to get to the bottom of this as soon as possible.'

'I'll just leave a note to let Watson know where we've gone.' Holmes scribbled a few lines on a piece of paper, left it on the table, and departed with Lestrade in tow.

As they sped off to the Kiiroashi Insurance Company, another cab slid into position behind them.

Lestrade's presence in the office produced the desired result and this time it was the general manager himself who brought out a bulky ledger. 'Which beneficiaries are you interested in, gentlemen?' he asked.

'The beneficiaries of the six men who recently took out life insurance policies and who have since died,' replied Holmes.

'Certainly, sir. Here are the pages you require.' The manager placed the open ledger on the table in front of them.

Lestrade bent over the list. After a moment he turned one page, and then another. 'So much for half of your theory, Holmes. There aren't six beneficiaries at all. Only one.'

'What! Let me see.' Holmes pulled the ledger towards him and flicked through the pages. Then he turned to Lestrade.

★   ★   ★

'You're right, I *was* mistaken. There is one and the same beneficiary in each case: the Kiiroashi Trust Fund.' Holmes addressed the manager, who had removed himself to his desk. 'Could you explain the nature of the Kiiroashi Trust Fund to us, please?'

'Yes, sir. It's a facility we offer all our clients, enabling them to invest any sum they wish and paying a very high rate of interest. It acts, in fact, as a private bank in which funds are safely deposited for later use.'

'And who controls the money invested

in the trust fund?'

'We divide our Fund into different categories, arranged alphabetically. Each category is controlled by a different financial adviser.' He paused to consult a document on his desk. 'Yes, each of these six men chose to invest in Category A, under the supervision of Mr A. P. Tolpin, one of our most respected advisers.'

'Could you tell us what amounts were invested in each case?' asked Holmes.

'One moment.' The manager consulted the document again. 'The sums were identical. The policies paid out twenty thousand pounds on the death of each man and this sum was transferred into the Fund as each death was confirmed. Let me make it a little clearer,' added the manager, rising from his desk. 'On taking out the policy, each of these six clients made the stipulation that on his death all of the twenty thousand pounds insured should immediately be transferred to Category A of our Trust Fund to avoid death duties and these wishes have been carried out.'

'So, Mr Tolpin controls a combined

total of a hundred and twenty thousand pounds now that all six clients are dead,' said Lestrade.

'That is so,' confirmed the manager.

Lestrade shook his head. 'I'll grant you this, Holmes. Your theory is becoming less and less fantastic by the minute.'

'Indeed. You see, my six beneficiaries did exist. They simply merged into one, that's all. Now, what about the other half of my theory?'

'Just a minute, let's not get ahead of ourselves.' Lestrade mopped his brow with a coloured handkerchief. 'What beats me is why six men — total strangers as far as we know — would all take out identical life insurance policies for the same amount almost at the same time, and then make over identical sums payable on death to the same category in the same trust fund?'

'And then conveniently die within weeks of each other,' added Holmes.

'There's a lot we don't understand yet about this whole sordid business.'

'You'll think I'm theorizing wildly again, no doubt, but I'm going to take the risk. I'll wager there's one controlling brain behind all this.'

'Not Moriarty again!'

'Yes, I'm convinced that Tolpin and Moriarty are one and the same person and, it's Moriarty's organisation that's in control. He'll be siphoning off the money from the account for his own devilish purposes even as we speak.'

Lestrade hesitated. 'I can't say I'm convinced, but — whoever is responsible — we are looking at a case of fraud at the very least, and there's something I can do about that.' He addressed the manager. 'Pending further investigations, I would strongly advise you to put an immediate stop on all payments from the Category A account. I have reason to believe that a fraudulent act has been perpetrated on the Company.' He turned back to Holmes. 'If it does turn out to be Moriarty, that should cut his profits down a little, I should hope.'

The manager looked aghast, but agreed to comply. 'By the way, Mr Holmes, you wanted to be informed of any additions to the list.'

'Well?'

'We received this one a short while ago.' He pushed a piece of paper across his desk.

Holmes took it. 'Lord Lexingham. This is the man I've been searching for, Lestrade, and it appears he has joined the ranks of the six. Did he take out his policy on the same terms as the others?' he asked the manager.

'It would seem so. Except for the beneficiary.'

'Who is the beneficiary this time?'

'Mr Sherlock Holmes.'

'What!'

The manager nodded. 'And, unusually, a note has been added to the transferred amount. It states: *in grateful recognition for services rendered.*'

Lestrade's eyebrows shot up in surprise.

Holmes stood still, his thin shoulders bowed over the document in his hand. Then he straightened up, his face ashen. He thanked the manager for his cooperation, took hold of Lestrade's arm, and propelled him from the room. Once they were outside he stopped, facing Lestrade with a grim expression on his lean features. 'Two things follow from this startling revelation. Firstly, it confirms my opinion that this whole business is Moriarty's work. This latest twist is obviously designed to involve me in the fraud conspiracy and damage my reputation in the eyes of the police. Secondly, it forces me to revise my opinion on the disappearance of Lord Lexingham.'

'You mean his life is clearly in danger now his name is on the list?'

'No, I do not think he has been marked out for death like the others. The note clearly shows he is in Moriarty's employ and has been used as a decoy, leading me on a false trail to my own ultimate disgrace.'

'You'd better explain yourself, Holmes. This is getting beyond me.'

'Moriarty's aim all along has been to make me appear guilty of collusion by associating my name with that of the Trust, as you have just seen. Everything that's happened — from the moment Lady Lexingham came to visit me, and including the six deaths and the insurance swindle — has been carefully planned to put me out of action while he completes preparations for an ingenious crime, which I shall be helpless to prevent.'

'I don't understand how what you've just told me could possibly *put you out of action*.'

'I'm now apparently assisting a criminal gang and Moriarty is counting on you to arrest me on suspicion.'

'Well I won't, knowing your record as I do.'

'How will your superiors react, when they hear you have failed to arrest the only suspect in a major fraud? You will have a lot of explaining to do. No, Moriarty has thought this through very thoroughly. You simply have to do your duty. There is no other way. However, you will have the satisfaction of knowing that, for once, Moriarty's and my wishes coincide.'

Lestrade looked completely taken aback. 'We're talking about your arrest here, Holmes. How can that be something you want to happen?'

'Once I am arrested — and you and I can interpret that in any way we like, as long as it looks official to your superiors and the outside world — Moriarty will feel free to carry out whatever devilry he's planning at this very moment. Overconfidence may cause him to show his hand sooner than he might otherwise have done, which will give us time to act. There's another advantage, too. I'll have a much freer hand for my investigations, because Moran won't be dogging my every step.'

It was Lestrade's turn to look a little more relaxed. 'I'm glad you're on the side of the law, Holmes. You'd make a formidable opponent with that devious mind of yours. A spot of house arrest should do the trick, I think. That will give us the flexibility we need.'

'The vital element is publicity. Make sure you let all the papers know the details of my arrest. Moriarty must be left in no doubt that it's genuine. I'll leave you to it. In the mean time, I'm going to use my last few hours as a free man to return to Beechcroft Manor. I have some rather pertinent questions to put to Lady Lexingham.'

So saying, he hailed a passing cab, and sped off to Baker Street.

Holmes arrived as Watson was about to enter the house. He called out to him from the cab: 'It will save time, Watson, if you join me. I'm on my way to Beechcroft Manor again and I'll explain as we go.'

Watson climbed aboard and the cab set off. 'Never a dull moment, eh, Holmes? Why Beechcroft again? Something must have happened.'

Holmes apprised him of all he had found out about the Trust and the resulting developments.

'I'd love to have seen Lestrade's face, when you told him he had to arrest you.'

'Yes, he was rather alarmed, but he soon came round to my point of view. Now, you have news for me, I imagine.'

'They were very cooperative at the Registrar's. I was allowed access to the medical records, but they all proved negative, I'm afraid. Death from natural causes every time.'

'We really need evidence, concrete evidence that arsenic has been used, but that's going to be difficult to obtain, unless . . . ' Holmes voice faded away and his face took on the dreamy look which meant he was totally absorbed in the solution to a problem.

Soon the cab pulled into the long, tree-lined entrance to Beechcroft Manor. Dusk was falling and Holmes and Watson expected to see the lamps burning in the windows of the house. All was dark, however. Only the dull outline of the house emerged from the gloom and a strange, deserted atmosphere pervaded the entire place. Holmes asked the driver to wait, while he and Watson went up to the front door. There was no response to Holmes' knocking and a rapid inspection of all the windows on the ground floor revealed nothing. The house appeared to be well and truly deserted and had taken on a neglected appearance.

'We're wasting our time here,' said Holmes. 'We can do nothing more tonight. I suggest we come back tomorrow in daylight and try to find out what's going on.'

Watson agreed and they headed back to Baker Street.

Later that same evening Moran was summoned to an urgent meeting with Moriarty. By the time he arrived, Moriarty had already received news that Holmes had been arrested and he was jubilant. 'No more need to follow Holmes. We all know exactly where he is now.'

Moran looked relieved. 'You mean I can begin my proper assignment, then?'

'That's exactly why I called you in. You're to start right away. The task should be completed by about noon tomorrow, I reckon, at which time you will switch to your major assignment, compared with which everything else will seem a mere distraction.' He rubbed his hands together, and picked up an envelope from the table. 'Full details. Jack and his gang will make contact with you as arranged. Best of luck to you.'

Moran took the envelope, thanked him, and returned home. He packed a small valise and rode a cab to the corner of Salisbury Terrace in Whitechapel, a cul-de-sac of elegant detached houses. He walked briskly along to number eight, the home of a Mr Smithson, a prominent City banker.

It was a calm evening with only occasional glimmers of moonlight through low banks of cloud. Moran went past the front of the house, looking for signs of any windows left slightly open. All seemed secure, so he crept along the path to the side. A window on the ground floor looked as if it hadn't been completely fastened. Moran continued to the back of the premises, and silently climbed over the wall into the garden. The window was indeed open and it was the work of a moment for Moran to climb in.

He found himself in a long corridor with several doors leading off from it. He was looking for Smithson's study. From the floor plan Moriarty had provided, it seemed to be the one at the very end of the corridor. Moran went up to the door, turned the handle very slowly, and pushed. Moran slipped into the study silently. He closed the door, removed a dark lantern from his valise, and lit it. A mahogany writing desk stood in one corner of the study and he hoped it would contain what he was looking for. As expected, it was locked, but Moran had come equipped with a small, pouch of tools for dealing with this kind of emergency. He had the desktop open in a few seconds and was about to start rummaging through the papers when he heard the sound of a footstep in the corridor.

He pushed the slide across the front of his lantern, pulled down the desk lid, and tiptoed over to hide behind the curtains. He looked down at the lantern and hoped the smell of the hot metal would not give him away. Through the gap in the curtains Moran could just make out the figure of a man in a dressing gown entering the room. It was probably Smithson himself.

The man turned up the gas lamp and seemed to be looking for a book in one of the cases lining the walls. He soon found the volume he wanted and turned to walk towards the door. As he reached it, he paused, came back into the room, and walked up to the desk.

Moran's heart was in his mouth.

Smithson took out his key to open the

desk. Surprised when it wouldn't work, he pulled open the lid. He cursed his servant, selected a document, and locked the desktop. Then he turned down the lamp and left the room.

Moran breathed a sigh of relief, but waited a while before emerging from behind the curtains. He slid back the cover on his lantern, unlocked the desk again, and found the papers he wanted. He put them in his valise, locked the desk, closed his lantern, and left the room. He exited the house the same way he had entered, with no trouble at all.

It was long after midnight before Moran arrived in Baker Street, but his night's work had scarcely begun. He spread the Smithson papers out of his table. Each of them contained examples of Smithson's signature and Moran had only a few hours to learn how to imitate it. He had to be able to reproduce it so well that he could pass himself off as Smithson at the insurance company's office. A challenging task, but he knew he could do it. Six of his colleagues had already completed similar assignments, so failure was not an option. He hardly slept that night, but he had the satisfaction of knowing he would be able to present himself as Smithson in the morning.

* * *

Early the next morning Moran made his way to the Kiiroashi Insurance Company and asked for the life insurance section at the front desk. He was shown into a small office, where a clerk noted his personal details. 'How can I help you, Mr Smithson?'

'I should like to take out a policy paying twenty thousand pounds in the event of my death.'

'Certainly, sir, if you would just complete this form for me.' He handed Moran a small booklet, containing a comprehensive list of questions to which Moran provided the answers as speedily as he could. The address for correspondence he gave was 221C Baker Street.

'If you would sign on the last page, please.'

This was the moment Moran had been

awaiting with some trepidation. It was all very well to produce an accurate imitation of a signature in the quiet of one's room, but to do so under the critical eye of a clerk was another matter. Moran coughed to clear his throat, gave his moustache a nervous pull, and put pen to paper. It was perfect. He pushed the booklet over to the clerk.

'Thank you, sir.' The clerk scrutinised the document.

'I would like to make one stipulation,' said Moran. 'Death duties on an estate as large as mine would be crippling for my family, so I want to take measures to reduce them. It would help me to do this if I could have the sum payable on my death transferred to the Kiiroashi Trust Fund Category A.'

'That will be in order, sir. Just complete this codicil and your wishes will be carried out.'

Moran did as instructed and handed back the paper.

'Thank you, Mr Smithson. We will be writing to you to confirm this transaction, at which time you will be expected to make an initial payment on the policy.' The clerk stood up and held out his hand. Moran shook it, said goodbye, and left.

He had one more thing to do, before heading for home — the second part of his assignment. He had to leave a message for the servant in Moriarty's pay at Smithson's residence to inform him the policy had been taken out.

Moran was soon back at Salisbury Terrace, but this time he walked boldly up to the front door. He handed a sealed envelope containing a coded message to the footman and asked for it to be delivered to the person whose name was on the envelope. He was assured it would be done. His assignment complete, Moran returned to Baker Street, satisfied with his work and ready to study the details of his next assignment, on which Moriarty set such great store.

* * *

Holmes and Watson rose early in preparation for their return to Beechcroft Manor. No police guard had yet appeared outside the house, so there was nothing to prevent them leaving right after breakfast. The contrast with what they had found on the previous evening could not have been greater. The house and grounds were a veritable hive of activity. Gardeners were cutting the lawns, digging the flowerbeds, and trimming the topiary. Windows and doors were wide open and servants could be seen scurrying past on their domestic duties.

Holmes handed his card to the footman and he and Watson were soon shown into the morning room. A dapper, middle-aged man came forward to greet them, pulling on a suede jacket. 'Good morning. My name's Lexingham. How can I be of assistance, gentlemen?'

Holmes introduced himself and Watson. 'Lord Lexingham?' he asked.

'Yes, that's me.' Lexingham looked puzzled.

'Forgive me, sir. I had not expected — '

'Us to be back yet,' broke in Lexingham. 'Well, we came back this very morning. We cut short our holiday because Lady Lexingham hasn't been very well.'

'Your Lordship has not been in

residence for some time, then?'

'No, we closed up the house when we left, two weeks ago.'

'Then who were the people living here when Watson and I called to see Lady Lexingham?'

Lexingham frowned. 'You must be mistaken, Mr Holmes. There couldn't have been anyone here. As I told you, the house was closed up.'

At that moment the door opened and a handsome figure of a woman in a pale lavender morning dress entered.

'Ah, come and meet Mr Holmes and Dr Watson, my dear. They are under the delusion that you received them in this house quite recently.'

Lady Lexingham greeted them politely. 'As my husband will no doubt have told you, we have been away for the past two weeks.'

'Then I must inform you that someone has taken advantage of your absence to fill your house with servants and personate you, Your Ladyship,' said Holmes.

'Why would anyone want to do that?' she asked in amazement.

'I shall make it my business to find out.' Holmes explained exactly what had happened, while they had been away.

'Astonishing,' exclaimed Lady Lexingham when he had finished, 'I thought that kind of thing happened only in the cheaper kind of fiction.'

'I assure you this is a deadly serious matter, Your Ladyship, and I will not rest until I have cleared the whole matter up.'

'We shall be most interested to hear the results of your investigations, Mr Holmes,' said Lord Lexingham. 'If we can be of any help — '

'While I am here, would you permit me a further look at the grounds?'

'Certainly. Do whatever you feel is necessary. Good morning, gentlemen.' He pulled a bell cord and the footman came in to show Holmes and Watson to the door. They made their farewells and left the house for the familiar path.

'What do you make of that?' asked Watson

'It is quite clear that Moriarty has been determined to keep me distracted so that I remain unaware of his real purpose.' Holmes struck his forehead with the palm of his right hand in frustration. 'We've got to find out what it is before it's too late. There must be a clue somewhere. It's probably staring us in the face and we just can't see it.'

They had reached the shed at the end of the path. Holmes idly pushed open the door as they passed. Suddenly it was jerked inwards and a young man clutching a toolbox rushed out, almost knocking Holmes over in his eagerness to get away. Holmes regained his balance and sprinted off in pursuit. He seemed to gain on his quarry at first, but then the man scrambled over the wall at the end of the garden and was gone.

Panting, Watson arrived at Holmes' side.

'The fake Lord Lexingham,' Holmes gasped, short of breath himself. 'I recognised him from the portrait Lady Lexingham showed us. It would have been useful to have found out what he was doing here now the deception is over.' While he was speaking, his eyes fell upon the path along which the man had run. Traces of thick yellowish clay made an outline of his footprints. Holmes bent down and picked up some of the deposit, studying it carefully. 'A most unusual colour and texture. I'm sure I've seen it before, but — for the life of me — I can't think where. We can do no more here, Watson. It's back to Baker Street to reflect on the morning's events.'

★ ★ ★

For three days there were no further developments in the case. In fact, there were no visitors at all at 221B Baker Street. Holmes' arrest had been made official by the presence of a formidable-looking policeman, who paced up and down in front of the house. Such a prolonged period of inactivity proved as irksome as ever to Holmes. No matter how much Watson thought he had accustomed himself to Holmes' moods at such times, he was always relieved when something happened to break the monotony. He breathed a heartfelt sigh, therefore, when, shortly after lunch on the third day, there was a sharp knock on the door.

It was a messenger from the manager of the Kiiroashi Insurance Company. He handed Holmes a note informing him of a new name that had been added to the list, a Mr Smithson of 8 Salisbury Terrace, Whitechapel. The name had been entered four days ago, but a temporary clerk had not realized the importance of informing Holmes immediately. The messenger apologised for the delay and hoped it would not cause too much inconvenience.

Holmes dismissed him with no reply. He read the text carefully and waved the paper in delight. 'This is a real chance for us to clear up much that still eludes us. With luck we shall also be in time to save a man's life.' He was eager to be on the move again, but restricted by his house arrest.

'Watson, would you go and inform Lestrade about this latest development, please? Ask him to come back with you as a matter of urgency.'

Watson left at once and returned with Lestrade a half hour later. Lestrade took custody of Holmes from his police guard and hailed a four-wheeler. Holmes, Watson, and Lestrade departed from Baker Street for Salisbury Terrace, and Lestrade wasted no time in rapping on Smithson's door.

It was opened by a footman. 'Mr Smithson is unwell at the moment and is not seeing anyone.'

'This is an official police investigation. We must see him at once!'

The servant responded immediately, escorting the visitors to Smithson's bedroom. He lay in his bed, pale and drawn.

'Watson, do what you can to help him,' urged Holmes. 'Mr Smithson, my name is Sherlock Holmes and my colleague, Dr Watson, is about to examine you. Inspector Lestrade is here in his official capacity.'

Smithson lifted his head and turned a pair of bleary eyes towards Holmes. 'Very grateful you have come, gentlemen,' he wheezed. 'I haven't been at all well lately and my physician hasn't been able to do much for me, as you can see.' His head dropped back on the pillow with the effort of talking.

'Arsenic poisoning, without a doubt,'

whispered Watson to Holmes. 'You've got all the concrete proof you need right here. The symptoms are clearly evident.'

'Did you hear that, Lestrade? This is exactly the way the six died. I hope we're in time to prevent a seventh.'

'I'm going to give him the first dose of antidote.' Watson drew a small package and a syringe from his Gladstone bag. 'You have some poison in your body, Mr Smithson, and I'm going to give you an injection which will make you feel much better.' Smithson nodded weakly. 'There. That should begin to take effect very soon.'

It wasn't long before some of the pallor began to leave Smithson's cheeks and he appeared far more lucid.

'Can you hear me, Mr Smithson?' asked Holmes. 'Can you understand, what I'm saying?'

'Yes, yes I can,' he replied. 'Please carry on.'

'Thank you. We have reason to believe an attempt has been made on your life.'

'What! How can that be? I haven't an enemy in the world. I'm an ordinary family man with an unexceptional circle of acquaintances. It's impossible!'

'Tell me then, have you taken out a life insurance policy in the past week?'

'Certainly not. I already have adequate life cover.'

'I thought so. Someone has taken out a policy in your name and now you're being poisoned so they can benefit by your death.'

'This is incredible.' Smithson tried to sit up, but couldn't manage it. 'I've signed nothing of late for any insurance company.'

'Then an example of your signature was stolen and used to help personate you and take out a policy on your life.' Holmes spoke to Lestrade: 'That's how the other six policies were managed — forged signatures every time.' He turned back to Smithson. 'As to the matter of the poisoning, could you let the inspector have the names of all your servants, please? He will wish to question them.'

'There may well be a charge of attempted murder,' confirmed Lestrade.

'But all my servants have been with me

for years,' said Smithson. 'I'd trust them with my . . . ' He stopped. 'I'll do as you say, Mr Holmes.' He took a piece of paper from his bedside table, wrote some names on it, and gave it to Lestrade. His strength was returning quickly, and Watson helped him to sit up while Lestrade left to find the servants.

'I'm glad we came in time,' said Watson. 'I'll be calling in to visit you regularly until you are completely recovered. Inspector Lestrade will arrange for a policeman to keep you safe until he has cleared your staff of suspicion.'

Watson and Holmes said farewell, leaving Smithson to his recovery and Lestrade to his interrogations.

Holmes hailed a cab for Baker Street, and they climbed aboard. 'So, Watson, there you have it in a nutshell. That interview with Smithson made everything crystal clear. I think even Lestrade understands it now. None of the six men knew they had taken out an insurance policy, because they hadn't. Moriarty's henchmen, selected for their resemblance to the six no doubt, forged their

149

signatures from stolen documents. Once that was done they gave a signal to the servants in Moriarty's pay and the poisoning began.'

'Well done. It's all quite clear to me now. This will make a fascinating addition to my stories.'

'Don't write it up yet. We still don't know the end. Moriarty has a surprise planned for us, for which all that's happened has been but a diversion. There's no end to the deviousness of his criminal mind. Never underestimate him.' His brow furrowed. 'I shall give this a lot more thought tonight over a few pipes of shag.'

After they had returned to their rooms and refreshed themselves, Holmes settled down in his favourite chair, his elbows on his knees, as smoke rose from his clay pipe. Watson sat with a copy of the *Star*. He glanced over the headlines, but the events of the day seemed so mundane after what they had been through that he soon threw the paper aside. He took out his notebook and began to write a narrative of the case. When he began his description of the fake Lady Lexingham's visit to Baker Street, he stopped and put down his pen.

'No matter how false she turned out to be, I can't help hoping no harm came to her. She was as pretty as a picture, wasn't she, Holmes?' He peered over at his colleague through the dense clouds of smoke.

'What's that?' grunted Holmes without interest.

Watson repeated what he had said.

'I didn't notice.' Suddenly a change came over Holmes. 'What was that you said, *pretty as a picture*?' He leapt out of his chair. 'You've done it again, Watson! You've given me the clue I've been searching for.'

Watson scratched his head. 'What did I do, Holmes?'

'You said *picture*, and right away I remembered where I'd seen that yellowish clay. They're digging up the road alongside the National Gallery in Trafalgar Square — that's where it is.

That's our goal, Watson, and that's where Moriarty's great coup is to take place. The fake Lord Lexingham had obviously just come from there when we surprised him.'

'A great deduction, Holmes, but those excavations are likely to go on for some time. How are we going to find out when Moriarty plans to strike?'

Holmes' enthusiasm waned somewhat. 'You have a point, Watson. We'll need a lot of official police help and we've got to be absolutely sure of our facts before we call upon them.' He sat down heavily and stroked his chin. 'Do we know of anything unusual that's due to take place at the Gallery in the near future?'

Watson picked up the *Star*. 'There's a mention here of the official opening of the final stage of the Gallery's new wing. The ceremony is scheduled for tomorrow morning.'

'That's it! Moriarty will be using the ceremony as a cover for his activity — or he may be planning to disrupt it in some way. Whatever it may be, we've got to be on hand to try to prevent it. Would you go round to let Lestrade know our plan, please? Thank you. Ask him to send a large contingent of police to the Gallery in the meantime. They should be in plain clothes and distribute themselves as inconspicuously as possible to avoid alerting Moriarty's men — and Watson, I have a feeling you may need your service revolver before the night is out. Come back for me with Lestrade as soon as you can.'

Within an hour the three of them were in a cab racing towards the National Gallery, eagerly anticipating whatever the night would bring. It was quite dark when they arrived and the only occupants were the nightwatchman and half a dozen policemen in plainclothes. One of the policemen was sent to the curator's home to request his presence. Inside the building the silence was palpable, and no one interrupted it. After what seemed an interminable wait, the curator arrived, accompanied by Lestrade's man. Holmes explained his fears that there might be an attempt to steal one or more of the valuable paintings that night or during the opening ceremony in the morning. He proposed a tour of the galleries where the most valuable paintings were hung and asked Lestrade to instruct his constables to keep their eyes open for any signs of tunnelling through the walls and floors. The curator explained the layout of the Gallery and suggested visiting each of the four wings on the main floor together with the new wing, the final stage of which would be officially opened the next morning.

Holmes and Lestrade followed the curator, their eyes scouring the dark recesses of the galleries, where the gas lamps could not reach. Watson walked more slowly, taking the opportunity to admire the paintings as he went. It was the first time he had visited the Gallery and, in spite of the uncongenial circumstances, he appreciated having what amounted to a private viewing of a collection of great works of art from all over the world. He recognised one or two: Leonardo da Vinci's *Virgin of the Rocks* and Titian's *Bacchus and Ariadne*, for example.

'This is our most valuable painting,' said the curator. They had stopped in front of a Rubens, the magnificent *Massacre of the Innocents*. 'Its current estimated value is forty-nine million pounds.'

Holmes and Lestrade exchanged glances. Lestrade indicated to one of the constables to remain on guard. The curator pointed out other precious paintings in each gallery they went through, but there was no sign that any had been tampered with. Holmes and Lestrade were satisfied that at this stage, at any rate, there was no evidence that a gang was preparing to strike. After their tour, they all went into the curator's office and sat in the hard-backed chairs he provided.

'It seems we've come on the wrong night, Holmes,' said Lestrade.

'It's beginning to look like it. But all the signs pointed to tonight.' He leaned forward, resting his elbows on his knees and addressing the curator. 'Are you certain, from your extensive knowledge of the building, that you have detected nothing out of the ordinary tonight?'

'Nothing, all is as it should be.'

'Do you have anything unusual planned to coincide with the opening of the new wing?'

'Why, yes. A few days after the official

opening we are staging a major exhibition in the new wing to demonstrate its innovative design. A large number of masterworks on loan from the private collection of Lord Stockville of Harrow will be displayed.'

'Have they been delivered yet?' Holmes asked eagerly.

'No. They are being sent down tonight and will arrive in the early hours of the morning for added security. You see, Mr Holmes, the items are valued at millions of pounds.'

Holmes leaned forward and banged his fist on the curator's desk. 'That's it! My instinct was right. We couldn't discover anything suspicious in the galleries tonight, because there was nothing to discover. We were looking in the wrong place. Moriarty intends to steal the whole consignment the moment it arrives at the Gallery. What a coup that would be for him.'

The curator's face had turned the colour of chalk.

'You've got it, Holmes,' cried Lestrade, shaking him by the hand. 'Now,' he asked the curator, 'where exactly will your consignment be unloaded?' The man produced a map and indicated the precise location at the back of the Gallery. 'You'd better come and show me, so there's no possibility of a mistake. I'll arrange for reinforcements in a few minutes.' He and the curator went over to the door. 'Coming, Holmes? You've got to be in at the kill.'

'Of course,' replied Holmes. 'What about you, Watson?'

'If you don't mind, I wouldn't mind a rest. My leg is playing up rather badly tonight.'

'You have a good rest, old fellow. It seems as if there will be a few hours, before the consignment arrives, so I'll ask Lestrade to send a constable for you later.'

'Thank you.' Watson watched Holmes depart, stretched out his legs, and closed his eyes.

* * *

Watson felt his head jerk and realised he must have dozed off. He got up and turned round, expecting to see Holmes or Lestrade returning after their reconnaissance.

'Good evening, Dr Watson,' boomed out a powerful voice. 'You didn't expect to see me, eh?'

'Moran! A bad penny always turns up, they say.'

'No names, no pack-drill. Didn't know you were an art lover. Thought you were a far less sensitive soul — bit like me, as a matter of fact.'

'Well we know it's not culture that brings you here, but you've extended yourself a little too far this time. Holmes has got your measure all right.'

Moran threw his head back and laughed. 'Holmes is the last person I'm worried about at the moment.'

Watson glared at him. 'I wouldn't underestimate Holmes, if I were you. You did that once before, if I remember.'

'We'll see who is top dog when he comes in that door.' Moran gave a low whistle and several of his men came rushing in. 'Tie him up, Jack and put a cloth in his mouth. We don't want him giving the game away, do we?'

Despite his protests, Watson was roughly handled and tied to his chair with a stout piece of rope. Then his handkerchief was stuffed in his mouth to prevent him making a noise. At that moment the door opened and Lestrade and the curator entered. Lestrade stopped dead in his tracks.

'Come in, inspector,' drawled Moran. 'Do take a seat so I can truss you up like the good doctor.'

'You're under arrest, Moran' growled Lestrade.

'Not quite yet. I have a small task to carry out first and I don't wish to be disturbed.' He signalled to Jack. 'Would you escort these gentlemen to their chairs, please?'

Lestrade and the curator received the same treatment as Watson.

Moran nodded his approval at the neat row of prisoners. 'Very good. Now, where is Holmes? Ah, I think I hear his approach.' Moran was right.

The door opened again and Holmes entered. He, too, stopped dead, taking in the unusual scene.

'Out on bail, Mr Holmes? And so we meet again. This time, I think you will admit, I hold all the cards.'

Holmes leaned back against the door. 'So it would seem. Appearances, however, are notable for being cruelly deceptive, have you not found?'

'Not this time, Holmes.' Moran waved his hand towards his men. 'I have men ready to take care of any number of Lestrade's constables.'

'Really? I've just completed an extensive search of the building and found nobody.'

'That's what you must expect to find, when you look for my men.'

Holmes inclined his head. 'Then I must resign myself to joining my colleagues in that undignified state.'

'I'm afraid I must insist.' He signalled to Jack and his men and a few moments later Holmes became the fourth prisoner. 'It's the first time I've had the pleasure of the last word in our conversations. I shall relish this for a long time to come. Meanwhile, duty calls. Farewell, gentlemen.' He bowed his head in mock salute and led his men from the room

It was only when a constable released the four men some hours later that the full story emerged. Lestrade's force had been hopelessly outnumbered and had been overwhelmed when the consignment of paintings arrived. They watched helplessly as Moran's men commandeered the precious cargo and he and Jack drove off with it. The rest of the gang had dispersed and there was no sign of any of them when the police reinforcements finally arrived.

'So much for your men,' muttered Watson, stretching his aching joints.

The curator was beside himself. 'You knew what was going to happen, and where it was going to happen, and you still bungled it! The Gallery has lost millions of pounds and I want to know who is going to pay for it.'

Lestrade freed himself from a last knot, spat out some the remains of a cloth, and coughed. 'I did everything in my power, and that's all anyone can ask. As for compensation, I still have every hope that we will succeed in tracing the stolen articles.'

'You're very quiet, Holmes,' remarked Watson, watching his friend smooth out the wrinkles in his lapels.

'What's done is done. The important thing to remember is that we all did our best, but it just wasn't good enough on this occasion. This is no time for recriminations.'

'That's all very well for you to say,' groaned the curator, wringing his hands. 'You haven't got to face my Board of Trustees and try to explain the loss. I tell you, I'll probably have to resign.'

Holmes placed a hand on his shoulder. 'Don't take it to heart. They're only paintings. No life was lost. There's always another day.'

'Only paintings! How can you be so confoundedly complacent?'

Holmes smiled sympathetically. 'I suggest you take me literally and wait for another day. And I see it's getting light outside, so you haven't long to wait.'

'Wait for what?'

'For your second delivery, of course,' replied Holmes.

'What are you talking about? I didn't arrange for a second delivery.'

'No, but I did, on your behalf.'

A stunned silence followed Holmes' remark.

Watson spoke first. 'This is no joking matter, Holmes.'

'You'd better explain yourself,' said Lestrade. 'You're holding something back and you owe us all an explanation.'

'I'm talking about the consignment containing the genuine paintings.' He paused to let the full implication of his words sink in. 'The one that Moran and his men got away with contains nothing but a load of worthless daubs that Lord Stockville sent at my suggestion. The genuine paintings are on their way here now under heavy armed guard. They should arrive within the next hour.'

'But how did you manage to warn Lord Stockville in time?' asked Watson.

'It was just too quiet in and around the Gallery for my liking, so I slipped out and sent Lord Stockville a telegram, explaining the whole situation. No doubt he complied fully, with his own property at stake.'

Watson could hardly believe his ears. 'A brilliant coup!'

The curator was fairly dancing with glee. 'It's a tremendous thing you have done for us, Mr Holmes. How could I have doubted your abilities? My trustees will be overjoyed and will certainly be in touch with you to express their gratitude.'

'Watson is the one who deserves your gratitude. Without his eye for beauty, we might never have been here at all.'

'You really are remarkable, Holmes,' said Lestrade. 'Congratulations. You have certainly saved our skins today. There's just one thing lacking to make this a perfect piece of detective work — to put the icing on the cake, as it were.'

'Oh, what's that?'

'Moran has eluded me on this occasion and I'd like to return a little of his hospitality. You wouldn't know where his regular haunts are, would you?'

'Try Baker Street.'

'Baker Street?' Lestrade's bushy eyebrows merged in a straight line. 'I don't understand.'

'He's our neighbour. He lives at 221C.'

'Sleeping with the enemy, eh?'

'It has its uses,' replied Holmes. 'I don't suppose he'll be returning there now, but you might trace his whereabouts by following anyone who comes to clear his apartment for him.'

'An excellent idea. I need to question him about those arsenic murders.'

'My view is that those crimes will never be solved. They'll remain on record as *death from natural causes*, I'm afraid. Moriarty will have made sure that all the perpetrators are long gone.' Holmes walked to the door. 'You can take some comfort from the fact that Moran won't have a very pleasant time of it when Moriarty has a look at that consignment. 'Coming, Watson?'

'Agreed, Holmes. 'What about you, Lestrade? You must be exhausted.'

'No, I prefer to wait, until the new consignment arrives, just to make sure.'

The curator looked up from his desk. 'Thank you, Inspector and my heartfelt thanks to you, Mr Holmes, for your remarkable intervention.'

'All in a night's work,' said Holmes. 'I wish you good morning, gentlemen.' And with a cheery wave of his hand, he was gone.

THE END

We do hope that you have enjoyed reading this large print book.

Did you know that all of our titles are available for purchase?

We publish a wide range of high quality large print books including:

Romances, Mysteries, Classics
General Fiction
Non Fiction and Westerns

Special interest titles available in large print are:

The Little Oxford Dictionary
Music Book, Song Book
Hymn Book, Service Book

Also available from us courtesy of Oxford University Press:

Young Readers' Dictionary
(large print edition)
Young Readers' Thesaurus
(large print edition)

For further information or a free brochure, please contact us at:
Ulverscroft Large Print Books Ltd.,
The Green, Bradgate Road, Anstey,
Leicester, LE7 7FU, England.
Tel: (00 44) **0116 236 4325**
Fax: (00 44) **0116 234 0205**

GUILTY AS CHARGED

Philip E. High

A self-confessed murderer recounts the events that led up to an apparently unprovoked attack; a gruesome murder scene holds nasty surprises for the investigating officers; a man makes what amounts to a deal with the devil — and pays the price; caught up in events beyond his control, a bit-part player in a wider drama has his guardian angel to thank for his survival . . . These, and other stories of the strange and unaccountable, make up this collection from author Philip E. High.